I0534439

Spanked
Real Stories

Gabriella Luciano

American Taboo Press
New York — Los Angeles

Author's Note

The act of spanking is tied up in so many emotional, psychological and physical dimensions that it is impossible to distill the whole world of getting a good ass smacking into simple statements. Yet, it is possible to take the broad array of women who have either gotten disciplined in a very memorable way in the past, or simply love to get their butts spanked a deep shade of red during sexual play in the present, and let them speak for themselves. For a number of years, as part of a post-graduate level research study into spanking and its effects, I got the chance to speak intimately with women who either were at the receiving end of unforgettable spankings or badly craved to be spanked as part of a deeper need to be desired in a very physical way by men. Although I could not publish these confessions in a formal academic study or research journal, the emotional truth and sexual honesty of these women, I felt, needed to be shown the light of day.

The women agreed to tell me their stories and desires in intimate detail as long as I kept their identities anonymous. I talked to hundreds and hundreds of women from across the country who I had met through friends, research connections, colleagues, online dating sites, in spanking fetish forums, via personal ads and even in person at bars and parties. The stories collected here are chosen from the vast array of confessions due to their unique qualities. There were many similar stories but the ones printed here really stuck in my mind as being especially exemplary of women with deep desires to be spanked by men due to powerful events or people in their lives.

Miranda T., *Cambridge, MA*

Q: So tell me about your experiences getting spanked.

Miranda: I've always been intensely reticent and kind of socially awkward. In high school, I was a bona fide nerd but as I matured in my early twenties in college, I started to gain more confidence. My body developed late and I ended up with really perky breasts and what guys would later call a very spankable bottom. It was my saving grace in the game of physical attraction. Yet, because I was still so socially inept, I channeled all my energy into academics. By the time I was 25, I was already a teaching assistant for a professor at a liberal arts college in New Hampshire. But halfway into the first semester, he took a sudden leave of absence and that was when I met Jacob.

Q: Who is Jacob?

Miranda: He replaced the previous professor. He was in his early thirties and had a pure New England prep school look to him. He had these bright blue eyes and a very rigid perspective of academia. He had studied the Classics, spoke four languages, was a Fulbright scholar and was a rising star in his field. He was very intimidating to say the least.

Q: How so?

Miranda: He nit-picked through every single paper I graded, grilled me about my educational background and generally made me feel like I didn't match up to him. I was also highly attracted to him and would fumble through my sentences every time I spoke to him. I felt like a fawning student in awe of the cool, know-it-all professor. Sometimes when he spoke to me, I would just start daydreaming about having some obscene unhinged fling with him.

Q: So what happened?

Miranda: I was in his office one day grading papers with him. It was a Saturday afternoon so there weren't many students or teachers in the building. Our exchanges had become more casual and he liked to joke with me about being the "naughty prodigy" because I was so young but still made silly mistakes. So, he was checking through an essay that I had graded and he told me that I had missed something. I inquired about what I had overlooked and he unexpectedly told me to come over to his desk to read it again. He gave me a sharp knowing look that seemed to insinuate something more than the grading of the paper.

I thought he might have noticed that I was trying to eye him from the moment I had come in. His very presence made me so anxious that I had to hide the goosebumps that radiated across every inch of my flesh. He seemed larger than life to me and he definitely dressed the part of some kind of movieland teacher with his charcoal-colored tweed jacket, his perfectly starched white shirt and his stiff designer jeans. When he lectured in class, the sound of the hard leather soles of his dress shoes clacking against the floor as he walked back and forth behind the podium made me shudder in sensuous revelry.

Anyway, so I stood up and walked around to his side of the desk, and then bent over to read the part he indicated. I was leaning over right next to him, just a few inches from where he sat in his immense wooden chair. I was wearing a pink skirt that was kind of short and I noticed right away out of the corner of my eye that he was glancing at me while I was reading. I think he could see that I was aroused just by being this close to him. I realized what I had missed and swiftly apologized for it. He replied in a firm tone, "Don't let it happen again, Miranda," and then suddenly gave me a light slap on my butt out of nowhere.

I was in utter shock that he would touch me like that. I made an "oh" noise of surprise, stood up straight and looked back at him. My face must have been crimson red and I grinned in uncomfortable embarrassment. He gave me that knowing, confident look he was always bestowing on me and then he smiled back. It was so arousing yet at the same time I felt a bit guilty that I let him cross that line of professional conduct. I guess I should have stormed out of there and filed a complaint of sexual misconduct, but it was the last thing I wanted to do. You could say my wetness was my personal acquiescence of consent.

Q: So then what happened?

Miranda: Without the slightest hesitation, he told me to read it out loud, word for word. My hand was almost shaking with nervous excitement when I reached down to pick up the paper. Then he unexpectedly stood up, took a hold of my hand and pressed it to his desk. I couldn't believe that he was suddenly being that intimate with me. It seemed to come out of nowhere, yet in retrospect he had caught me flirtatiously eyeing him so many times that he probably knew exactly what he could do to me. Then he ordered me in a very firm manner to "bend over and read it."

My heart was racing and I laughed awkwardly. I glanced back at him in uncertainty, nearly frozen in fear. He took his other hand and calmly pressed my back forward, bending me over toward the paper. He sharply repeated his command to read it. The moment was so erotic and overwhelming. I began to read the passage quoted in the paper. It was from Ovid's *Ars Amatoria,* a book about how to seduce women and prevent others from stealing them. After I read the first few words, he arched his hand behind me and spanked me on the butt again.

Q: How did you react?

Miranda: I stopped reading but he immediately told me to continue. I feverishly began to read again. He stood up and I felt him lift up my skirt. My heart jumped but I didn't try to stop him. I thought I was going to faint. He pulled up my skirt like it was a totally normal thing to do. I guess I should have been outraged that he would be so presumptuous about being outright physical with me but I wasn't at all. My voice, though, cracked in fits of anxiety as I tried to keep reading. I could feel my bare thighs exposed and it took all my energy just to swallow. The moment was so intoxicating. He still had one hand holding my hand against his desk when he swung his other hand to spank me. It struck one of my cheeks at the edge of my underwear so that the ends of his fingers slapped against my bare flesh. The sound filled the room and I glanced at the door to make sure it was fully closed.

He simply told me to keep reading and his hand tightened over my hand. I still remember the exact line I read next: "What you blush to tell, is the most important part of the whole matter." I began to read the line and I felt him delicately pull my underwear up between my cheeks so my bare ass was almost entirely exposed. I stopped in the middle of the line and he told me to start again. I began the line again as his palm landed hard on my bare butt. My voice broke into a high-pitch mumble and he told me once again to read the line from the beginning. His body was hovering just over mine as he continued to spank me over and over as I tried to read the entire line without stopping.

Q: How were you feeling?

Miranda: I could hardly think straight. My thoughts and emotions were whirling inside me like a tornado. I had never expected him to do such a thing, but it was absolutely exhilarating. I had fantasized about him many times before but this was absolutely real. It was so intimate being in his office but it also felt completely forbidden and taboo. I was terrified that someone outside his door could hear but he didn't seem the least bit worried. He didn't hesitate for a single moment. He was tremendously unwavering as he told me to read it again and spanked me even harder. I finally was able to calm down enough to read the passage in its entirety. I felt him straighten my underwear back over my bare butt and pull my skirt back down. Then he casually released his grip on my hand.

Q: What happened after that?

Miranda: He told me that was sufficient and that I could return to grading papers. I stood up and awkwardly walked back around his desk to my chair. I sat down and nervously glanced up at him. My body was practically shaking. He smiled deviously at me, knowing how much I liked what had just happened. My face must have been a bright shade of red and I had begun to lightly perspire.

Q: Did he say anything to you?

Miranda: Yes. He asked me in a very formal manner, "Do you have any objections to being spanked for future mistakes, Miranda?" I looked down in embarrassment and then back up at him. The way he said it was incredibly proper but also very warm, inviting and sexy as hell. I cleared my throat and tried to pretend like I had to think about my answer. It was as if he was asking me a benign question about office hours or something like that. I simply replied accordingly: "No, that would be fine." There was so much restraint in both of our voices that I thought I was going to burst. He casually grinned, nodded his head in confirmation and then went back to grading papers. I did the same, or at least, I tried to do the same.

Q: What do you mean?

Miranda: I couldn't even focus on a single thing in front of me. After a couple of minutes, I excused myself to go to the restroom. My legs were shaking as I walked down the empty hall. When I got to the safety of the women's room, I lifted up my skirt in front of the mirror to look at my thoroughly reddened butt. The mere sight of it was so thrilling. I felt the front of my panties and they were totally wet. I was so turned on that I wanted to touch myself right then and there. I slipped into one of the bathroom stalls and locked it. I placed my back on the closed metal door, slid my hand beneath my underwear and started to fondle myself. I must have had an orgasm in like two minutes. I just re-imagined the scene over and over in my head, still reading the line to myself.

Q: So what happened after that incident?

Miranda: Nothing else that day, but there was a class a few days later and he was giving his regular lecture in the large auditorium. I would always attend the class and sit to his side at my desk. I would typically be taking notes until he gave me a task such as passing out reading material. Well, I was supposed to have brought a batch of graded essays to class to return to the students but I had left them in my car. Toward the end of class, he told the students I would now return the papers and I realized I did not have them. I was just so nervous and forgetful around him. So I ran to my car to get the papers and quickly returned. When I got back to the class, he looked at me and then announced to the class, "My naughty prodigy will now return your papers." I couldn't believe he said it in those words. All the students chuckled and my face turned bright red. After that day, he would simply address me as the "naughty prodigy" in front of the whole class. Students must have known something was going on.

Q: How did that make you feel?

Miranda: I felt it was a bit humiliating, almost demeaning, but afterward I would imagine prancing up and down the steps of the auditorium in my skirt and sweater as he called me his "naughty prodigy" and I would get so aroused. I think my underwear was wet with excitement by the end of nearly every class.

Q: Did he spank you again?

Miranda: Yes. After class, he told me to stop by his house that evening for my spanking for forgetting the papers. He wrote down his address on a slip of paper and gave it to me. It felt like we were crossing a line by meeting at his house. I even looked up my work contract, wondering if it was allowable for staff to be involved.

Q: Was it?

Miranda: I couldn't find anything forbidding it and I was afraid to ask, of course.

Q: So did you go to his house that night?

Miranda: Yes. I was so nervous and it felt so illicit. I must have changed clothes a dozen times. I mean, how is one supposed to dress for a spanking? I ended up deciding on a gunmetal blue pencil skirt and a white blouse without a bra. It seemed to elicit thoughts of kinky spanking scenarios to me. I wore these frilly white panties underneath that were like tight little shorts. When I got there, I parked a few houses away from his house just in case someone saw my car. I don't know why. When I rang his doorbell and he opened the door, I could smell that he was cooking. He invited me in and asked me if I had eaten dinner yet. I told him that I had not and asked me if I'd like to join him. I casually agreed like it was no big deal but my mind was racing with the thought of the evening turning into something else. He was wearing dark jeans and a tan sweater with a light blue dress shirt underneath. He looked so damn alluring.

I started to follow him toward the kitchen but then he suddenly turned back toward me. He said, "Let's get the spanking out of the way then." He turned everything formal in this decisive way, like it was completely normal that his teaching assistant was to be given a spanking before sitting down for dinner. He instructed me to go to his home office, pointing me toward an open door on the other side of the living room. He saw me smile and he said, "Miranda, this is your second infraction. You'll be getting it quite hard this time." My heart jumped as his face turned more serious. Then he told me, "Assume the position over my desk with your panties down." He said it in the same formal manner and then turned to go back to the kitchen.

My heart was beating a million times a second as I walked to his office. I turned on the light and looked at his desk. It was a large antique oak desk with papers and books stacked on it. I nervously put my hands under my skirt and pulled down my panties to my thighs. I bent over his desk and reached back to flip my skirt up over onto my back. I spread my palms across the smooth lacquered surface of the desk and waited. I could hear him in the kitchen cooking but I couldn't see him. I could only imagine how I must have looked. I have never felt so exposed. At least fifteen minutes must have passed while I patiently waited bent over in that position.

Finally, I heard the echoing thud of his footsteps as he walked across the hardwood floor toward me. I stretched out my fingers across the desk and straightened my legs. The anticipation was the most excruciating thing of all.

When he walked into the room, he simply said, "Miranda, you already know what you did, so I will not waste any time lecturing you." I just nervously replied, "Okay." His hand came down hard across my bare cheek and I jerked from the sudden contact. Then, he began to forcefully spank me on both cheeks in wickedly fast bursts. I bent my legs to try and absorb the swats, but he just pushed my back down against the desk and kept spanking me harder and harder. I started to vigorously breathe in and out to help me take the pain but he only continued to furiously spank me. I could feel the perspiration start to form on my forehead.

He was really slapping my bare cheeks quite harshly and I thought I was going to faint for a moment. This went on for a good five minutes without stopping. I kept thinking he was going to pause to rest but he didn't. Finally, I just couldn't take it anymore and I burst out in a moment of panic, "Please. That's enough. I can't take anymore." He gave me a few more hard sharp smacks and then he finally ceased. He calmly said to me, "Come in for dinner after you've recovered." Then he simply walked out of the room.

Q: What happened after that?

Miranda: It was the strangest series of events. I pulled my underwear back up and stood up straight while I got my bearings. I took a few minutes to gather my composure and then went into the kitchen. He smiled at me like everything was completely normal and asked me if I would like a glass of wine. It was as if the spanking hadn't even happened. He started chatting about a movie that he had just seen as he poured the glass of tempranillo for me. We sat down to eat and had a really romantic dinner. We talked about school and politics and the news and art – everything except for the spanking. It was if he completely separated out from his mind what he had just done. I wanted to ask him about it but I didn't. It gave an erotic intensity to the dinner. I could still feel the warm pain radiating from underneath my skirt.

After we finished eating, we were just sitting there drinking wine. We had been casually flirting with each other during dinner and it grew more explicit. There was a tangible sexual tension in the air, and finally, he just reached over and kissed me. I kissed him back deeply and that triggered both of our impulses. We devoured each other. He pulled me to him and I climbed on top of his lap, wrapping my legs around his body. He was very aggressive and I loved it.

He had his hands all over my body. Suddenly he stood up, lifting me into the air and holding onto me with one arm. He reached behind me and swiped the plates to the side of the table, and then set me down on the end of it. He slipped his hand between my thighs and just ripped my panties down. I watched him undo his belt and in a matter of seconds, I had my back on the table and he was fucking me. It was so uncontrolled and intense. I think both of us wanted it from the moment I walked in. We ended up on the floor and we made love for quite a while. It was so unbelievably good. It was all I could think about for days afterward.

Q: Did he spank you during sex?

Miranda: No, not once. I had expected him to but he didn't.

Q: And did he after that night?

Miranda: Yes, he began to spank me regularly. There was this total separation between his spankings and our romantic relationship. It was as if one part of him was my disciplinary mentor and another part of him was my clandestine lover. But I could never totally separate the two. Every time I earned a spanking, it hurt like hell but I would think about having sex with him for the rest of the day. I loved how he kept them very formal. It made me feel like his naughty student who needed to learn the hard way. He never tried to make the spankings sexual, but he had to know how much they turned me on. In retrospect, I think he did it intentionally. He knew that it made me want him so much more because he was so restrained about it.

Q: What did he spank you for in particular?

Miranda: Many, many things. He was extremely meticulous and detailed with everything – my teacher's assistant duties, my thesis work, grading assignments, being on time, reading books he recommended…things like that. He liked to make me read from the Ovid book in Latin whenever I was at his house. That was the one thing in which the disciplinary and the sexual seemed to cross. He had an old school desk at his house—the kind with the little desk attached to the seat. Yet, there was no back on the seat part of it. It was as if it had been intentionally removed. He would make me sit down at it with my leggings and underwear pulled down so my bare butt was completely exposed. He had this old ruler that was made from this hard wood. Whenever I would mispronounce the Latin words, he would strike it across my bare skin.

It was so, so arousing sitting there reading erotic poetry in Latin and being spanked with his ruler. I learned nearly the whole book by heart but ended up with these long red marks across my cheeks by the end of every lesson. After we were done with the session, I would throw myself at him and we would make love. It was the only time I was allowed to do that after being disciplined. It was our little thing.

Q: How did things go from there?

Miranda: Wonderful. We started to grow closer and closer as the semester passed. I felt like I was living a naughty hidden existence that made the position altogether more thrilling. I adored how much attention he paid to me as his naughty prodigy and it seemed like he could never be strict enough. Apart from the discipline and the nights of intense sex, we actually connected quite well despite the age difference. When I wasn't getting spanked for some infraction, I loved to just cuddle in bed with him and ask him a million questions. I realized then that I definitely adored being treated like a babygirl and had probably always been attracted to older men. I felt like he was this strong wise presence and he welcomed taking that role. I knew that he really did care for me beyond the kinky aspect of it, and we were certainly both very kinky in a kind of furtive way.

It was such an oddly magical and transformative time. I adored being the younger girl who felt protected and looked after. I loved to kiss and cuddle under the covers like a romantic, and at the same time, I was enthralled in being the woman engulfed in a whole new world of raw manly sex and endless conversations that flowed through the whole spectrum of academia and humanity.

I loved the warm cocoon-like existence we inhabited. I would sometimes lounge around his house in the afternoons like a kitten waiting for him to come back from campus. He'd open up the front door to see me on my hands and knees on his living room floor, completely naked except for his ruler clenched between my teeth. He'd just smirk at me in this very restrained manner, even though I knew deep down he was fiendishly excited, and then stroll over and take me by the back of my hair and lead me to his bedroom. It was pure bliss. I wish it could have lasted forever.

Q: How long did it last?

Miranda: About a year. He ended up taking a position at another college and had to move. We tried to keep seeing each other but the distance became too difficult and the intensity of the affair started to wane. I think that the spankings were more a part of the relationship than we wanted to admit. He was the first older man who I had been with and I was really enamored with the idea of being his naughty girl. Eventually, the fantasy started to wear off, I was too young for him and there were only the spankings that remained. That's not to say that I didn't like them. I loved them. It still gets me wet just thinking about the first time he bent me over and spanked me while I read erotic poetry to him in Latin. It's like a permanent impression on my mind and on my ass. Even to this day, I still fantasize about it constantly.

Riley C., *Seattle, WA*

Q: So tell me about your spanking experience.

Riley: Well, I've always been a bit of a brat and I love when a man puts me over his knee to set me straight, yet it had been quite a while since I had gotten a good hard spanking. I had been living in Seattle for a number of years and was thoroughly bored with and burnt out by my job. I had moved from Texas just to take the position as the head of sales at this renowned tech firm because they had made me an incredibly lucrative offer. I was enamored with the city but I rarely had any time to truly enjoy it. Not only was I working a ridiculous number of hours, but almost all of my colleagues were diehard techies with who I had little in common apart from the job. Even when I had the time to go out on dates, I found it almost impossible to meet anyone truly compatible who wasn't all wrapped up in his own tech-related venture. It was tech, tech, tech…every which way I looked and I was sick of it.

When it comes down to it, I'm really a feisty small-town Texas girl at heart who likes to be out free in the wild and loves her men to be even wilder. Plus, I tend to be quite bossy at work but crave to be on the opposite side of the power dynamic in any personal relationship. I just wasn't finding any of that. I was seriously considering putting in my resignation when the most unexpected chain of events occurred.

Q: Events?

Riley: They were events to me, especially at the time and they were each rather serendipitous. It all began when I needed to make a rare visit to our packaging department.

There was an unusual shortage of product containers that was preventing us from making shipments of items that had already been sold weeks before. I was genuinely irate that we were not making our numbers because of some stupid supply chain issue with containerboard. I mean how fricking hard can it be to make more cardboard?

So just as I am strutting into the warehouse ready to throw a fit, I notice this man standing there waiting who looked completely out of place. He was wearing thick, heavy jeans and had the sleeves of his blue plaid shirt rolled up tight on his muscular forearms. It seemed as if he had just walked straight out of the woods and he was not happy about being there. That was my first very provocative impression of Kingston.

Q: Kingston? Who is he?

Riley: He is the CEO of the local lumber and paper company that supplies all of our packaging needs. I had no idea that there was still such a person as a lumberman but there he was in the living flesh. I later learned that he had recently taken over the operations of the family business from his father. I stopped briefly to talk to our shipping director about the holdup and he motioned toward Kingston, telling me: "That's the man you need to talk to. He says you called him a dozen times about getting the 'goddamn boxes' you ordered."

My heart nearly skipped a beat. After not making any headway with our packaging orders from the company, I demanded to speak to whoever was in charge of the mess. I had left a series of heated messages, each one nastier than the last. When I turned to look at Kingston, I felt his stern blue eyes pierce right through me. I did my best to bury my emotions and casually walked up to him to greet him. I extended my hand toward him and he slowly unhinged his crossed arms to take my hand into his. His grip was unusually firm and his huge palm practically engulfed my entire hand.

Q: So how did the conversation go?

Riley: It went everywhere expect where I expected it to go. After we introduced ourselves, I immediately asked him when the delay was going to be fixed. He gave me this condescending smirk and then said to me: "Listen, miss. I understand you people think the whole world runs by pressing buttons on phones and keyboards, but when there isn't enough recycled materials these 'goddamn boxes' you want come from real trees and you don't tell a tree how fast to grow."

I naively protested, telling him: "Of course not, but why don't you just cut down more trees when there's an obvious surge in market demand?"

He burst into a fit of laughter and shook his head. Then he said to me: "Miss, pardon my blunt honesty, but you have no idea how the lumber and paper industry works and if I knew you better I'd take you out to the woodshed myself and teach you about respecting nature the old-fashioned way."

When his brazen words sunk in, my thoughts started whirling in all directions. I couldn't believe he was speaking to me like that. I knew at that moment that he was of an entirely different breed of man than the guys I had grown accustomed to in the city. For a split second, I felt like I was back in Texas listening to some cavalier wildcatter.

"Excuse me?" I replied incredulously, even though my emotions had been stoked into a ribald frenzy.

"You heard me," he countered. "We have a contract and you'll get your 'goddamn boxes' as soon as we can make them. But if you need to see for yourself, instead of leaving me a bunch of sassy messages, you should come up to the mill and I'll show you."

I suddenly felt like I had spoken really haughtily and apologized for the messages. I told him that would be fine and we shook hands once again. He turned to leave when it struck me that I couldn't possibly let this conversation be the end of things with him.

"One second," I called out to him. He stopped and waited to hear what I had to say. "I would like to see for myself." He wasn't expecting this response and there was a moment of silence. He eyed me up and down as if he was sizing me up, and then he started to stroke his chin while he thought about my proposition.

"Come by tomorrow afternoon," he told me. "I'm free around five. Does that work?"

I responded that that would work. He gave me one last incredulous look with a slight grin on his face and then he left.

Q: And what exactly made you take him up on his offer?

Riley: It was his whole demeanor. Everything about him was so raw and unfiltered. When he told me that he would take me out to the woodshed himself, that unleashed a whole flood of memories and desires. It wasn't just that I had actually been taken out to the woodshed as a girl, but that he was the kind of bold straight-talking man who really got me going. All I could think about after he left was him making me "respect nature the old-fashioned way". I couldn't wait to see what was going to happen.

Q: And what did happen?

Riley: I drove out to the mill the next day. It was nearly a two-hour drive and situated far off the highway at the edge of the state forest. It was quite a trek and I started asking myself why I was even doing this. When I arrived, it was late and it seemed as if the last handful of workers were on their way out. I entered the main office but it was dark and empty. There was no one even at the reception desk. Suddenly I heard a voice and looked down the unlit hall to my right. There was a ray of light coming from a half-opened door at the far end. As I made my way toward it, I heard Kingston's voice. He was talking to someone on the phone.

When he saw me appear at the slit in the doorway, he glanced up. He motioned for me to come in. As he finished the conversation, I glanced around his office. It was like a sanctuary of wood. On the dark paneled walls various cuts of pine wood were hung. Some of them were fresh samples and others were historically dated. Other various pieces of all shapes and sizes were scattered all around the room. The stark scent of the freshly cut wood was intoxicating.

He quickly told the person he was talking to that he'd have to call them back in the morning and then hung up the phone. He said that he didn't think I was going to show and I apologized for my late arrival, confessing to him that

I hadn't realized how long of a drive it would be. There was a moment of silence as he just nodded and stared at me.

"So what exactly would you like me to show you, miss, to prove we're at full capacity?" he asked me.

I told him that he could just call me Riley and he repeated his question, addressing me as Ms. Riley. I was trying to conjure up some valid reason for coming all the way there but I really didn't have one. Plus, I couldn't take my eyes off his enormous forearms and his work-worn hands resting on his desk. I decided to just let things fly.

"I believe you told me that you were going to teach me about respecting nature the old-fashioned way," I suggestively taunted him. I stared directly at him as if I was posing the question as a challenge. There was just something about him that made me want to get under his skin in a million naughty ways.

A few seconds passed as he pondered my abrupt flirtation and then he stood up. He moved around his desk and approached me.

"Ms. Riley, I prefer to keep business separate from pleasure if you know what I mean," he explained.

"I see," I replied. "Perhaps then our company needs to find another supplier who can deliver what we want," I baited him.

He moved closer to me so our faces were barely a couple of feet apart. I could suddenly feel my heart beating heavily in my chest.

"Ms. Riley, you got quite the sassy mouth on you," he told me.

I eyed him for a moment as I playfully bit my lip. "So what are you going to do about it?" I daringly asked him. He stepped even closer to me. I could smell the earthy scent of sawdust on his clothes. "I thought you said you were going to take me to the woodshed," I added.

Without the slightest hesitation, he responded: "There's plenty of wood right here if it's an old-fashioned whipping you're asking for." He reached up and wrapped his hand around the back of my neck. The tension between us was so heavy I could barely stand it. "Is that what you're asking for?"

I don't think I had ever been so riled up in my life. Without even thinking I told him: "I don't think you're man enough to really do it."

Before I knew what was happening, he reach over my shoulder and pushed the door so it slammed shut. I felt myself being whisked across the room and practically flung over the top of his desk. My hands fell flat on the smooth lacquered surface as I tried to gain my composure. I glanced over my shoulder and saw that he had already picked up a broad thin piece of fresh pine wood that was the size of a paddle. For a second I thought I might have asked for more than I could handle, but I figured it was too late for me to back down now.

I felt him take hold of the bottom of my skirt and roughly toss it over my back. The feeling of having my bare ass exposed made everything starkly real, but what he did next was absolutely unforgettable to this day.

Q: What do you mean? What happened?

Riley: He reached over to pick something up off his desk. I quickly realized it was a knife. I started to jump up in fright but he pushed me back down firmly and told me to relax. My heart was racing like mad when I felt him grab hold of my underwear and cut them right off in one sharp motion. He dropped them onto the desk in front of me and then put the knife back down from where he had gotten it. I let out a sigh of relief.

"There's a little souvenir for you," he joked. "And now I'm going to give you the big souvenir."

I was in such a state I couldn't even speak. A few seconds passed as I heard him fumbling with something behind me. After he had sliced my underwear right off of me, I couldn't even begin to imagine what was next. I was almost relieved when I realized he was only holding his mobile phone which he placed on the desk in front of me. He tapped the screen and I unexpectedly heard the sound of my own voice. It was the first of the many messages I had left him.

I was listening so closely to the expletive-filled rant, feeling utterly embarrassed, that I was totally unprepared when the thin plank of wood smacked against my bare cheeks. I gasped in shock and clutched at the desk to hold myself still. Not a second passed before he spanked me with it again, and then again. I exhaled in and out in rapid bursts as the sensation sent shivers through my whole body.

He told me: "Just relax, Riley. There are plenty more messages to hear. You did say I should call you by your first name didn't you?"

I replied: "You can call me by any name you want."

He took the flat strip of wood and whipped it across my bare ass a few more times. "How about I call you my sassy little bitch?" he asked me.

I told him: "You'll have to make me your sassy little bitch."

He took the wood to me a half-dozen more times and then said: "I think I might do just that."

The intense chemistry between us was unreal. The more I taunted him, the harder he spanked me. Each stroke stung but the warm pain was getting me inexplicably aroused. Each time he stopped, the only sound in the room was my own voice ranting and raving on his phone. I had lost count of how many messages had played but when he heard another disrespectful comment erupt from the speakerphone, he'd give me a "no you didn't just say that" warning and start to spank me once again in a fury. I think I could have taken his lickings all night long.

Q: How long did it go on like that?

Riley: I have no idea. I completely lost track of time. I realized at one point that the phone messages had ceased but that he was still paddling me incessantly. By that time, in between the spankings, he would run his hand over my bare cheeks, tenderly touching the inflamed skin on one side and then the other. My flesh was so sensitive that the feeling of his huge palms caressing me sent shivers of pleasure through every part of me. Eventually, the last time he did it, I pushed myself back toward him until I felt his thighs touch mine. I couldn't take it anymore. I repeatedly pressed my bare ass against him, bouncing back and forth over and over until he finally just put down the strip of wood and undid his pants. He took me vigorously right there over his desk. I must have had an orgasm in minutes but he fucked me right through it and had his way with me for the longest time. It was so damn good.

Q: And after?

Riley: He sat down on his chair in exhaustion and I crawled on top of his lap. He joked with me that I sure knew how to get a man riled up and I told him I had never met a man who made me want to rile up so badly. Like I said, we just have unbelievably good chemistry. It really was the most unexpected chain of events.

Q: But I mean after that night, did you see him again?

Riley: Of course. I made weekly visits to his lumber company and he began to come into the city to see me on weekends. We became seriously involved with each other almost immediately. I told my boss that I was working on the packaging problem which gave me an excuse to go see him and re-enact our initial rendezvous over and over. I feel so lucky that such odd circumstances brought us together. He can't get enough of my bratty attitude and he relishes dishing out spankings with every makeshift wooden paddle in his office.

He's also really quite the possessive type and likes to manhandle me in all sorts of ways. Even when he comes into the city and we go for a stroll through the market at Pike Place, he'll openly fondle my butt in front of everyone. He loves for me to know that my ass is his. When he whispers in my ear to ask me if I'm his sassy little bitch, it gets me so wet to tell him that I am. It doesn't take long for me to start mouthing off to him and for him to drag me to the gentleman's restroom to give me a hard bare-ass spanking bent over the sink.

Q: What is it exactly that makes you like to act like a brat?

Riley: It's just how my personality has always been. I'm feisty to the core and love to test my man so he gets physical with me. I like to have my way in general and be very spoiled, but when a guy tells me no and then puts me in my place, it is such an incredible turn-on. I guess it's my way of getting attention and feeling like he really cares. I know it's a bit immature but that's half the thrill of it. There's nothing like a man showing me how much stronger he is and then backing it up by whipping my butt as if I'm just a naughty little girl to him. I fucking love it.

Q: So things are still going well?

Riley: Absolutely. I mean we're still getting to know each other, but I'm madly in love with him. We are such different people as individuals but together we are a perfect match. I mean even apart from all the spankings and the whole physical attraction, we connect like old friends. I just can't believe how it all came about.

Mackenzie K., *Bellaire, TX*

Q: So tell me about your spanking experiences.

Mackenzie: My experiences? That's a long tale to tell and we'd have to travel down even longer personal avenues and a few grander boulevards of a complicated life. Also, I keep that part of my life almost entirely private. Only my fiancé knows the full extent of my cravings.

Q: Private? Why is that?

Mackenzie: It just always has been. It's my own little world of escape that I can let myself go completely free. It gives me this redemptive release that nothing else can. There are so many other intermingled feelings and fetishes that go along with it, but to be honest I've had a thing for spanking since as far back as I can remember.

Q: You mean you got it growing up as well?

Mackenzie: I guess you could say that. I got it a handful of times from others, but it was more an internal discovery of its power over me at a very young age. I actually spanked myself a hundred times more than I was ever spanked by my mother or father. The sights and rumors of others getting it probably had a more robust effect on how I felt about it. I was definitely stricter on myself than my parents ever were. I did gymnastics as a child for years and one time after I had a bad practice, I went home and locked myself in the bathroom. I turned the shower on so no one could hear and spanked myself as hard as I could while watching it all happen in the mirror. I was absolutely captivated by the sharp stinging sensation and the sight of my own reddened butt.

I felt like I should have done better on this gymnastics routine and I deserved to be punished. Even at that young age, I was the sternest judge of my behavior. I am some kind of born perfectionist and I yearned to discipline my body for what my mind was sure it thought it could do. I tried to swat myself so hard and for so long until I couldn't take it anymore. I was never strong enough, though, and later on I started using a large flat-backed wooden hairbrush. I experimented with other implements as well. No one had any idea that I was beating my own butt for years and years. That's how it all started.

When my parents divorced, this need to self-discipline only grew larger. It was the one thing that genuinely grounded me. My childhood was very chaotic for quite a while but I always had spanking to hold on to. It never left me. It was always there for me. Plus, I think I am just wired to crave physical contact.

Q: So when did you start getting it from others?

Mackenzie: I got it from my first serious boyfriend in high school and a number of other guys, but I always had to explicitly ask them to do it. Some of them indulged me while others thought I was kind of a freak for wanting them to spank me so much. It made me start hiding the fact that I needed it so badly. It would make me blatantly act out with boyfriends so they would get so furious with me that they would willingly put me over their lap and spank my butt raw. Over the years, though, it was rare to find anyone mutually compatible who wanted to give them to me as endlessly as I craved them. I kind of buried my deviant needs for a while or indulged myself with a hard hairbrush whipping. I figured that as time went on that spanking would just be my own little private kink and that the larger realms of sex and serious relationships would take over my thoughts.

Q: But they didn't?

Mackenzie: Nope. I mean they did in a way but they also amplified and exaggerated my longing for spanking to be thoroughly intertwined in any serious relationship I had. Also, after a number of years toiling away in the corporate world of advertising, I was going a bit crazy. I get outright obsessive with my ambitions and become my own worst enemy when it comes to trying to micromanage the entire universe. Over the years, spanking has become so tied up in my need to escape to a carefree world in which someone else entirely takes over my say in anything. I think if I hadn't met my fiancé I would have driven myself completely mad. He imagines that I'm this wunderkind who just naturally gets a million different things done every day. In reality, I'm a desperate mess flying around like a tornado in all directions. If I didn't have him to take hold of me and give me the big, bad world of spankings and strict rules that he gives me, I would probably be in an asylum.

Q: And how did that come about?

Mackenzie: I actually met him at a work conference I was at for a weekend in Nashville. I don't think I would have ever been as overtly open with him as I was but the fact that I was out of town and not really expecting to ever see him again made me act a bit reckless. We were having drinks at the hotel bar with a bunch of other colleagues. Mason was actually on my list of people who I was supposed to try to land as a client. He's probably a decade older than me as well. He owns this company that brands itself as a kind of old-school men's way of living with its products. A lot of ad agencies want their business.

The conversation started out very professional but somehow turned more personal when it was just the two of us talking alone. In the middle of a heated exchange, I blurted out: "Well if our agency does not actually deliver on its promises, you can just whip my butt for lying to you and I'll fix it." I meant to say it in a metaphorical way but I think my true cravings just slipped out of my subconscious. In any case, the moment I saw his reaction, I knew he was one of them.

Q: One of who?

Mackenzie: A devout spanker – someone who is outright possessed by the impulse to smack his girl's ass. I would have never guessed it if I hadn't made that remark and had seen the look on his face. He has this aura about him that is so relaxed and gentle. He exudes a quiet confidence, but it is only one side of him. Another side of him – a very significant side – is this formidable six-foot stud of a man who will beat my butt senseless if I cross a single line he tells me not to cross.

So, he immediately called me out on my brazen promise and told me that I needed to prove to him that I had no issue taking a sound spanking if it was deserved.

Q: And what did you say?

Mackenzie: I hesitated for a second and started fidgeting about while I was figuring out how to respond. I was unsure about abruptly putting myself out there like that in a work situation. Finally, I just asked him when exactly he'd like me to prove it to him. He responded that he wanted proof right that very moment. Our eyes met and we both knew exactly what that meant. It was such a tense moment. I could feel the sweat form on my palms. I knew I had to go through with it. So, I glanced around the bar to make sure no one was watching, and then I slipped him my hotel room key card and told him I'd be waiting for him. It all happened so fast. One moment we were heavily engaged in business and the next moment we were completely lost in each other's physical cravings.

I scurried to my room and had barely finished preparing myself when I heard him at the door. I was wearing a gray business skirt and a white blouse, along with black heels. I perched myself at the end of the hotel bed on my hands and knees, with my skirt unzipped and pulled down to my thighs. I had on a tiny light pink g-string with a little bow. When I had put it on that morning, I had no idea that it would be his very first impression of my perverted little ass.

After he entered and closed the door, he didn't even say another word to me. He simply placed one of his hands on the small of my back and started to methodically spank me with the other hand in slow heavy whacks. It was like love at first touch. I glanced back at him, gave him a playful giggle and then leaned forward with my arms outstretched and my face flat on the bed. Neither one of us spoke to each other the entire time. There was only a long pleasurable dialogue between his weighty smacks and my muffled grunts, between his measured pauses and my labored breathing, and between his varied grips of my body and my obscene utterances that seemed to go on and on and on. It felt so weirdly natural and like a strangely perfect way to meet.

Q: And after?

Mackenzie: We talked incessantly for half the night while I cuddled my body all over his. We didn't even kiss much less have sex. The conversation was that good. I was taken aback by how warm and curious he was. All the other men who I had met up to that point who were forthright about liking to spank women were very domineering or self-centered jerks. Mason is completely the opposite. He is so open-minded that when he does take a firm stance with me, it is jarring. I know there is no way I am getting out of a blistering ass whipping.

Q: So I take it you got his business?

Mackenzie: Well, no. I mean I guess I could have gotten it, but we were way too much into each other. I would have been questioned at work as soon as people found out we were seeing each other. I mean it didn't really matter in the end because after having a long-distance relationship for about a year, I quit my job and moved in with him. I found another position and we have been happily involved ever since.

Q: And now you're engaged to be married?

Mackenzie: Yes, but neither one of us really cares too much about rushing into a marriage. We have a uniquely open relationship and don't really place much meaning on ceremonial events. Our undeniable connection and our intimate explorations are like daily marriages to us. I wake up with a much stronger craving for him to put his heavy loving hand on my naughty ass rather than to put a wedding ring on my finger. The balance in life that he gives me is so precious. I still try to work like a maniac but now he tells me unequivocally when I'm getting carried away and that I need to be done with work for the day.

He is like that with everything I need to be taken to task on – my sassy mouth, being late, not being communicative with certain things…he has particular rules for me for just about everything I have issues with. That is on top of his own demands and urges. Occasionally, he'll get in a mood some weeks and just want to come home from work every day and relieve his stress by taking his strap to my bare ass until it is bright pink. I don't complain.

Yet, the most profound change in my life since the day I met him was how much I can completely let go and trust that he won't judge me. All the freaky, deviant urges that I keep private from everyone else in the world are wholly public to him.

Q: Such as?

Mackenzie: Mmmm…I don't really want to confess too many details but a lot more taboo scenarios. Like I mentioned, I really crave physical contact and sometimes I like him to be really rough with me. He'll slap me across the face for talking back or just slap me repeatedly while he's manhandling me and forcing his cock down my throat over and over until I'm covered in drool. He'll tie me up as well and take a horsewhip to me on certain occasions.

We also do a lot of role playing that acts on the fact that he is older than I am. After being at work all day and having to be the ambitious take-charge adult that the world demands, I adore throwing myself into a make-believe world of acting like an innocent but naughty little girl who needs her daddy to teach her all of life's lessons. I love to pretend I am so terribly naïve as he makes me do the most depraved sexual acts and tells me that that's what a good girl does for her daddy. We get quite taboo.

We feel like we could explore anything with each other and even trust each other to be with other partners. I think we're unique in that way. There's no jealousy at all because we're so honest about it. I really can't imagine how it could be any better. We've actually been talking about having kids and the only reason we're putting it off a bit is because we know how much more chaotic and complicated our lives will become. I just want to cling to this part of my life for a little while longer as I am so deeply aware it is something special and want to savor every last second of it.

Scarlett H., *Marina Del Rey, CA*

Q: So tell me about your experiences getting spanked.

Scarlett: Well, I had this boyfriend who always had this thing for the woman being on top when we had sex. He thought it was the preeminent sexual position. Plus, he was really kinky in general and our relationship was exceptionally physical from the onset. He was very much an alpha male type through and through. He worked in finance and liked to play as hard as he worked. The very first time we had sex in fact, he was on top of me but he quickly dropped to his back and swung me on top of him. At the beginning, I was just casually riding him, but then he ordered me to "squat fuck" him. I didn't even know what he meant at first. He told me to turn around, get on my feet and squat down on his cock. I did as he asked me to do, but after only about a minute my legs started to get tired. Without any warning, he suddenly spanked one of my cheeks really hard with the thick palm of his hand. I whipped my head around and looked at him in shock.

He had such a look of extreme pleasure on his face. He was grinning at me and told me not to stop. When I turned back around, he immediately spanked my other cheek just as hard. He had never been so physically rough with me so I was a bit stunned to discover just how much it turned him on to smack my ass like that. It seemed like each time he spanked me, the harder his cock would get. He was really turned on by it which made me want to ride him up and down even more forcefully. It was the first time anyone had made spanking such an intense part of having intercourse with me. In retrospect, it was just the beginning of my discovery that I really love both the sensation of getting spanked as well as how tremendously arousing it is for some men to do it. There's just this raw intensity of contact play. It's as if an ass is just made to get spanked. I mean it's the only part of a woman's body that a man can just smack as hard as he can and you just want him to do it again and again.

Q: So what happened after that?

Scarlett: Well I kept squatting up and down on his cock like a little jackhammer. Every time I started to get tired and slowed down, he would spank me again and again. It reinvigorated me and I would get a new burst of erotic energy. Eventually though, my legs were shaking from the fatigue and I had to stand up. He pushed me down off the end of the bed and told me to put my hands on the floor. I did and he grabbed me by my legs and pulled my hips around his thighs. He swiftly thrust himself into me and started swatting my ass again and again. It stung like hell but the pain was so damn arousing. I squeezed my thighs together and rode him like that. I felt like a wild animal with my ass in the air but the position was so fucking good. His cock was riding up and down against my clit while he spanked me furiously. I had a deep, moaning orgasm and was still horny for more but my legs got so tired I had to stop.

Q: And how did he react?

Scarlett: Well, he was disappointed how fatigued my legs got. He told me that from that point forward that I would be required to start working out more so I could squat fuck him all the time. At first I thought he was crazy but the next time I went to the gym, I started to get really into it. I did like a hundred squats and lunges and pelvic thrusts and every other glute-clenching exercise I could think of. I could barely walk the next day. He laughed at me because I couldn't do anything in bed because my legs hurt so badly.

Anyway, over the next few weeks, I really became obsessed with it. I mean I was in decent shape before, but I slowly became fixated with working out my legs and ass. I would sometimes go to the gym twice a day just to do dozens of various exercises that focused on building an Olympic-quality bubble butt. I even started running more and doing yoga as well. Each time I came back from the gym, he instructed me to pull down my workout tights so he could give me a proper inspection. If he thought I was making progress, he would give me a light smack and give me some "good girl" affirmation. If he thought I needed to work harder on it, he would spank me really hard. That would only turn me on though and we would start kissing and things just turned wildly physical from there.

I did, though, get better and better at squat fucking him. It became almost ritualistic. Sometimes when I came over to his place he would grab me by my hair and warn me that my ass better be prepped to worship his cock. I was like his little porno girl but I kind of loved how infatuated he was with my lean shapely booty. I could go for nearly ten minutes without stopping after a couple of months of working out. It just became this obsessive kinky turn-on to get spanked over and over while I rode him. Afterward, my ass would be glowing bright red and I would feel the warm pain radiating even the next day. It took on this special meaning apart from the larger complications of our relationship. It made me feel deliriously desired to such a degree that getting spanked became something I had to have in any relationship after him. I also simply loved how he got more and more turned on as I got more and more skilled at it.

Q: It sounds like it was a vital part of your connection with him.

Scarlett: It truly was, as strange as that sounds. I was always naturally into physical connection with guys but he probably brought out my full-blown spanking fetish. We both just got really into it. At one point, he bought me a bunch of extremely tight workout leggings to wear at the gym. I was so self-conscious wearing them. They completely rode up the crack of my butt cheeks and gave me a very explicit camel toe in the front. I must have looked like a slut. He would go to the gym with me and put me to work on the squat rack. A few times, toward the end of a hard set, he would give me a few hard slaps on my ass and tell me to give him three more reps. My face would turn red because I knew other people must have seen him do it or looked over to watch me, yet getting spanked publically was just another level of arousal for me.

When he wasn't at the gym with me, guys would approach me constantly. I mean, here's this woman in these really tight leggings doing nothing but exercises for her ass. I was just asking for the attention. One day, when I was changing clothes in the gym, I was standing in front of the mirror half-naked and this black girl passed by. She glanced at me and then made a joke about my cute bubble butt. It was amusing but at the same time it was like true validation. I looked in the mirror again and it struck me how much my body had changed. I went home that day and just gyrated my ass over and over in front of my boyfriend like a drunken stripper. He spanked me so hard that time that my ass hurt for days. We had other kinds of sex, but nothing did it for both of us better than when I squat fucked him to a hard spanking. I even started to dress differently to accentuate my curves. I wore obscenely tight jeans and thin leggings that stretched so snuggly around my cheeks that it was as if I was wearing nothing at all. I became utterly consumed by it.

Q: What happened with the relationship from there?

Scarlett: Well, our relationship began to run its course. We had less and less to talk about, so in response, we just got more and more intense with the spanking. He would make me walk around his apartment naked, would bend me over the kitchen table before breakfast and spank me, he would spank me in public, and so on.

We went to Vegas one weekend for a kind of a pleasure trip. He bought me a bunch of really skimpy bathing suits – thongs, g-strings, tight short-shorts. When we went to the pool, I couldn't leave him for a second without being accosted by a hundred guys. I had pushed the workouts to the extreme and had this perfectly tight model-quality butt. One day, before we went to the pool, he bent me over and just gave me a really hard spanking. I was protesting like hell because I knew it was going to show. Then, I realized that that was his intention. I looked in the mirror and my ass was bright red from the spanking. I refused to leave the room but he just grabbed me and spanked me more.

He finally convinced me to go down to the pool. I wore a little sarong on the way there, but the moment I pulled it off, all eyes were on my ass. It gradually became a real turn-on, though, to be so exhibitionistic about my spanked cheeks. My boyfriend sent me to the bar to get drinks and I had to stroll the entire length of the pool to get there. Every guy must have been looking at me in my tiny white g-string with my ass bright red and thinking that I was a serious freak. By the time I got back to the chaise lounge, I was so horny. We went up to the room and I spent the rest of the evening squat fucking him. It was endless kinky experiences the whole time we were there. Being on vacation can really put you at ease in letting your slut out to play.

That was our last real weekend together. It just couldn't get better than that sexually and the rest of our relationship was getting very boring. Things had run their course. As much as I was into the physicality of it, I really craved true mental and intellectual stimulation in the end. We agreed on a mutual break-up but we met regularly after that for a quick fuck here and there. Every time I go to the gym to this day, all I think about is squatting and getting spanked. I think I need therapy. One thing that came out of it, though, was that I now know how to drive any man wild. The moment I turn around and start to methodically squat up and down on my current boyfriend, squeezing his cock with my cunt like a vise grip, he just goes absolutely mad. I have to ask him to spank me harder, though, because he's not nearly as physical as my ex. Some guys love to spank and most others just kind of like it. You can never find everything in one man, of course, but I don't think I could ever have a serious long-term relationship with someone if they weren't open to giving my ass the proper attention it deserves.

Arianna M., *New York/Australia*

Q: Tell me about your experiences getting spanked.

Arianna: He was an older Australian man, I mean at least a few of years older than me. He lived on a neighboring ranch next to my parent's estate out on the edge of the outback. They had purchased the place from a family friend with the intent that it would be their retirement home. I had never even been to Australia even though my father was born there and had dual citizenship. It was a few months after they had purchased the place that I decided I would go visit. I had been living in New York and working a very stressful corporate job that required me to put in 60 or 70 hours a week. I needed the escape.

Q: Did you find it?

Arianna: (laughs) Well, I don't know if I found escape but I certainly found what it's like to get whipped out in parts of the rugged Australian territory where neighbors are few and far between.

Q: He whipped you?

Arianna: Actually, he used a carpet beater, but let me start from the beginning. I arrived at my parent's ranch with the intent to stay for a week. They had settled into the place, had begun to farm a number of crops they grew to supplement their income and had even purchased a few horses. I had grown up as a child in Kentucky so I was completely at home on top of a horse. So, two or three days into my vacation, I would ride the horse out to the far stretches of their property. They had acquired a couple thousand acres so their neighbors were literally miles away

43

from them. Well, one day I took the horse to the western edge of their property. My parents had told me that there was a man by the name of Ross Higgins who lived there. They told me they had only met him once or twice but he seemed to be an eclectic sort of frontiersman. He was divorced and spent most of his time overseeing his vast acreage of cotton crops.

Q: So what happened?

Arianna: It took me nearly a quarter of an hour just to make it to the property line which was marked with an old handmade wooden fence and a lot of barbed wire. I rode along the line until I made it to his place that was set near the edge of the main dirt road that divided the territory. As I approached his ranch house, the sight of his figure standing in the rear courtyard grew larger and larger. I could see that he was at work doing something but I could not see what he was doing. There was just this silhouette of a man on the landscape making a kind of swift motion with his upper body and the muffled sound of a harsh thud at the finish of the motion.

Q: A thud?

Arianna: Yes. It was only once I got close enough to his house that I saw that there were a half dozen large carpets hung over a clothesline and he was striking them with some sort of an object. I only half-recognized the object. I think I had seen it in a movie or something. I knew that it was called a carpet beater and that it was used to beat the dirt from the carpet in an age before there were such things as vacuums and steam cleaners. When I saw him viciously striking the thick pieces of fabric, it almost seemed cinematic. Plus, I guess I had always assumed that women had used them in their traditional domestic duties. To see a man using the wicker implement to strike the dirty rugs was disorienting at first, particularly since he had the look of a rugged outdoorsman. He was wearing a pair of thick tan dungarees but his deeply tanned chest was as bare as it could be. I pulled up my horse and just sat there watching him. The intensity with which he struck each carpet with the beater was very impressionable.

Q: How so?

Arianna: He would wind up like a baseball player getting ready to hit the ball out of the stadium. Every time he struck the beater against the carpet, he would hit it with the full force of his whole body. At times, it seemed as if he would catapult his feet right off the ground. There was such a violent intensity to it but at the same time it seemed very poetic and beautiful as I watched it from a distance.

Q: So what happened?

Arianna: I was just sitting on my horse watching him do his work, repeating the motion over and over, when he suddenly looked up in my direction. He must have felt that someone was watching him. He stopped and looked toward me. When he saw me, I felt my heart skip a beat. I really wasn't doing anything I wasn't supposed to be doing, but I think I had started to be more of a voyeur than an innocent stranger who happened to come upon him. It only took him a couple of seconds to motion me to ride down the length of the fence in his direction. I immediately led the horse down the line of the property as he casually walked to meet me. When I pulled the horse up in front of him, he eyed me for a moment to try to figure out who I was. He asked me if I worked for my parents and I told him that I was their daughter. He simply nodded up and down while he took stock of me. There was an intense visual exchange after I took a moment to ogle his body. He was a good number of years older than me, but still very fit with a strapping torso from, what I assumed, many hours and days of rugged labor. His thick brown hair was graying at the temples.

He asked me why I was watching him beat the carpets. I told him that I was American and that I had never seen anyone use a carpet beater. He still had it in his hand and I was covertly examining the woven design of the wicker implement. I made a comment that I thought women were the ones who typically use them and he immediately frowned at me. He told me he was divorced and his own daughter didn't have any clue how to properly beat a carpet. He said that it had to be struck with a certain force to displace the dirt from the tight fabric. He said it in such a technical way but it seemed so provocative in its erotic suggestiveness. Maybe that was just me. I don't know.

Q: So did something happen?

Arianna: Not then, no. We talked for some time. I asked him more about beating the carpets and he inquired about my visit to the country. There was definitely this strange connection between us. He was a bit irritated that I had come upon him unannounced but I could tell he was intrigued by this seemingly naïve American woman watching him from the edge of his property. He rested the wicker beater on his bare shoulder as he spoke to me like it was a hatchet or a baseball bat. He showed no shame or feelings of self-consciousness to the fact that he was violently beating these dirty carpets like a man possessed with an uncanny intent to purify them. After we talked for a bit, there was a lull in the conversation and he said he had to get back to his work. I wished him a good day and rode off towards my parent's place.

Q: And after?

Arianna: That night, I had some intense dreams but I could only remember fragments of them upon waking. Immediately after breakfast, I took one of the horses out again and headed straight toward his place. When I got there, it must still have been very early in the morning as the air was still a bit chilly. I expected somehow to find him in the same place where I had left him but not only was he not there, but the carpets had been taken back into the house. I hesitated for a moment but then noticed a light on in one of the windows of his ranch. I slowly rode up the length of the fence so I was just yards away from his dwelling. When I saw his bare body through one of the windows, I pulled up the horse and froze in place.

Maybe I wasn't used to the secluded nature provided by the vast distances between each house, but it seemed like he was on full display for me to watch. He had evidently just showered as he was toweling the water off of his body. He was stark naked and he rapidly wiped the moisture from his tanned skin with a white towel. My first instinct was to ride away but I was afraid that the noise from the horse would betray my presence. I remained as still as I could on my horse and ogled his body as he shimmied it dry. Suddenly, he made a quick motion toward the window to hang up the towel and he glanced out the window. Our eyes locked and his expression transformed into a look of shock and fury.

I didn't know what to do. I couldn't just ride away. Well, I guess I could have but I didn't. A few moments later, he stormed out of the back of his place wearing only his jeans and a pair of dark brown boots.

Q: And what did he do?

Arianna: He literally stomped across the distance from his back door to the spot where I rested at the edge of his property. He began to shout before he even reached me. At first, I could only hear random words from what he was saying. Not only because of the distance but because there was a steady breeze blowing. It was phrases like "how dare you?" and "who do you think you are?" and "you dirty little voyeur." It was that last one that really woke me up. I mean I was afraid from his reaction but when he called me a dirty little voyeur, that got my attention. I suddenly felt like I had committed a crime or something. I mean I had just ridden up to the edge of his property to see if he was beating the carpets again. I don't know why I thought he would be doing it the very next day, but I didn't mean to catch him in the nude.

So by the time he got to me, my heart was racing like crazy and I didn't know what he was going to do. His face was red with anger and he was still shouting at me in full fury. He finally told me to get down from the horse and I did. He immediately looked me up and down. I was wearing full leather chaps over my riding pants and I must have looked like some high-class equestrian snob to him. He demanded to know why I was peeping in his window and I tried to tell him that I didn't mean to. I was just there to watch him beat the carpets. He looked at me like I was some crazy American tourist who thought he was there just to give her an Australian outback show.

Q: Is that what he said?

Arianna: No, that's how he looked at me. What he said was that he was going to teach me what happens to "dirty little voyeurs." He told me to tie up my horse and "get my skinny ass" inside before he beat it right there. I didn't know what to do and I froze for a second. My parents had said he was eccentric but I didn't know if that meant he was dangerous. When I hesitated, he moved to step through the barbed wire fence to come toward me, and I quickly relented to his orders. I tied up my horse and ducked through the fence. He immediately grabbed my arm and led me towards his house. My mind began to race with the possibilities of what he was going to do. I mean, we were practically out there in the middle of nowhere. All he said was that he was going to teach me how he beat the dirt out of the carpets. I knew deep down that he meant he was going to do more than that.

Q: What do you mean? Why didn't you just leave?

Arianna: I don't really know. I could have just left, but I didn't. I felt like nothing really bad was going to happen and whatever did happen, no one would be able to see or hear way out there anyway. It was like I slipped into another zone of reality. This strapping Australian man had caught me peering through his window and was now roughly leading me into his house. It just felt like it was supposed to happen.

Q: And what did happen?

Arianna: He took me to the back courtyard of his house where he had been beating the carpets the day before. There were a number of nylon cords tied to metal poles over which he had laid the rugs. It looked very ramshackle like as if he had built them himself. When we got to them, he told me to lift my arms and wrap them around one of the lines. That was the point at which I felt he was a bit crazy. Well, I don't want to say crazy, but he had a certain pathological way of seeing things that included it making sense in his mind for making this American woman wrap her arms around his carpet hanging lines. I hesitated and he told me to get my arms up there. I glared out toward the prairie as if I was seeing if anyone was there. I mean I'd been living in the city. I wasn't used to risking myself like this without the safety of a cell phone call or a scream to someone passing by.

Q: So did you do what he asked you to?

Arianna: Yes. I think my arms were trembling but I made the leap of faith. I lifted my arms and wrapped them around the nylon cord so they were extended out in both directions. Then, he immediately told me he was going to beat the dirt right out of me and that he was going to teach me not to be a naughty little voyeur. I should have run away right there but, in retrospect, his words really turned me on. I had watched the sensual intensity in the way he used the carpet beater on the rugs and it seemed like there was just a whole world of emotion simmering underneath the violence. I turned my head back toward him as he went into the house. I still remember the sound of the screen door smacking loudly against the frame of the house. In a matter of seconds, he strutted back out with the carpet beater in his hand. It was the same one he had used the day before. It was a long wicker thing with a simple woven design at its end.

He approached me quickly and didn't give me any time to prepare really. He just told me he was going to beat the dirt out of me and I suddenly felt the harsh sting of the carpet beater strike my butt. It hurt like hell, even over the thickness of my jeans and I gasped in pain. He whipped it across my butt several more times and each time I could hear the whisking sound of it as it flew through the air. When it struck me, a cloud of dust was sent from the fabric of my jeans and quickly blew away in the brisk breeze. All I could think was how insane this moment was. He was beating me like a carpet and I kept my arms entwined in the nylon cord like I was supposed to be beaten like a carpet.

Q: Did he say anything?

Arianna: The first few times, no. He just did it. I had never been spanked for real up to this point except when just playing around sexually with boyfriends. This was for real. It hurt like hell, but I just gripped the cord in the palms of my hands to bear it. I never turned around or tried to resist. After he whipped it across my butt a few times, he started repeating: "I'm going to teach you how to get the dirt out, young lady." He said it over and over. Not only did it make me realize that he didn't even know my name but that he was obsessed in some deep way about getting the dirt out of what should be clean. I had talked to him briefly at our first meeting about his ex-wife and daughter but he didn't really seem like he wanted to provide intimate details about what happened. There was something about the carpet beating, I think, that helped him vent his emotions or relieve some deeper pain inside of him.

Q: How many times did he strike you with it?

Arianna: Probably ten times, and then he paused for a moment. I had gasped in pain each time that he did it but it definitely felt like just a preparation for something more intense. When he stopped, I glanced back at him but I didn't say anything. The whole experience felt so cathartic, like words didn't matter. When I looked back at him, he seemed to be just examining his work. It was as if he was seeing if he got all the dirt out. Then, he suddenly approached me and quickly reached around my waist. He immediately started unbuttoning my jeans. I should have been shocked, but like I said, it was all so strange for me to be out there in the middle of nowhere. I think my mind had been so trained, from living in the city, to always think about what others thought of me rather than what was actually happening to me. I don't know. I brought a lot of emotional baggage to the moment as well. I was so stressed at work and with my own relationship that I desired some kind of extreme release. Maybe all the stars were aligned to make it happen how it did.

Q: And how did it happen?

Arianna: He unbuttoned my jeans, button by button, and then pulled them down to my thighs. I mean he did it really, really quickly and in a rough sort of way. He certainly wasn't concerned about how I felt about it or about being delicate. I was still wearing my leather chaps which must have made the whole thing seem so graphic. I mean they were belted around my waist and covered the lengths of my legs, but they are made in such a way that if you happen not to be wearing anything else only your bare ass and bare front are left uncovered. But he could only pull down my jeans to the middle of my thighs without stopping to take them all the way off so he just tugged them down as far as they would go.

There was a brief moment of silence while he reached to pick up the carpet beater again. It gave me time to realize the insanity of the situation. I mean I could have just slipped my arms out of the cords and run away, but I didn't. I waited for him. It occurred to me how we were in this together. It was not so much that there was a deep connection between the two of us as much as we each had an uncontrollable urge to participate in the act. I know that sounds crazy...to participate in the beating of my bare ass in the middle of the Australian Outback, but that's what it was. We needed it deeply beyond any reasonable explanation.

Q: So did he give it to you?

Arianna: Yes. He told me that he was "going to beat the dirt right out of my body." It was pure mental delusion but I just listened to his words like I was watching a movie. He wasted no time in beginning the act. The first time I felt the sting of the hard wicker against my bare bottom, my body flinched and convulsed. Beads of sweat began to form on my forehead immediately. It was intense. I knew that old-fashioned Australians had punished their kids with these things, but I was shocked by the pain. I felt like some kind of martyr. Each time he whipped it across the thickness of my bare butt, the woven end of it struck both of my butt cheeks at the same time with a vicious force. After the first one, I gasped loudly in pain. After the next couple, I cried out from the pain and started mumbling to myself how badly it hurt. After the fifth or sixth stroke, tears began to stream down my cheeks and I was wailing in pain. I literally screamed out but it didn't matter. There was no one there to hear my cries except for him. I began to scream at the top of my lungs because I knew that there was not a single person who was going to come, not a single soul who would arrive and ask me why I was letting myself be whipped with a carpet beater by a total stranger.

The crazy thing was, and I don't know if I was just hallucinating, but I began to see clouds of dust blowing off of me each time he struck me. It was probably just the dirt on the ground or on the carpet beater, but in my frenzied state of mind, I imagined them coming right off my body. I'm sure I was just romanticizing his vision of beating the dirt from me, but that's what I saw at the time. Of course, sweat was beading from my forehead and I felt like I was about to faint from the pain, so perhaps I saw things that were not there at all.

Q: How did it end?

Arianna: I don't know how many times he whipped me with the carpet beater but I think my body started to become limp and I was just hanging onto the nylon cord with my arms to remain upright. I remember feeling like I was going in and out of consciousness. I would close my eyes and then open them again. When I felt an end to the rhythm he had used in the strokes, I opened them completely wide. He walked around to the front of me and stood a few inches from me. He told me that if he catches me again peeping in his window, he'll whip me bare. I had so totally submitted to his ritualistic spanking that I just nodded up and down. He passed from in front of me as quickly as he had appeared. A few seconds later, I heard his screen door slam behind me.

I took a few seconds to gather my composure and then slipped my arms from the nylon cord. There were deep marks on my skin that circled around the girth of my forearms. I shook them to try to get the blood to flow back into them as they were numb. I pulled my jeans back up, buttoned them and slowly walked back toward my horse. It all felt so unreal despite the real pain radiating from my butt. The day had hardly begun and here I was wiping the tears from my eyes after being senselessly whipped by a wicker carpet beater. I have never told anyone I know about the remotest detail of that day.

Q: Was that the end of it?

Arianna: Pretty much. I mean I was only there for a week. When I got home, I went to the bathroom and immediately pulled down my pants to look at the results of it all. My butt was not only bright pink but there were raw red markings from where the edge of the carpet beater had struck me particularly hard. The skin was raised in places and welted up. My entire bare ass was warm to the touch and there was a deep pain that radiated from every inch of it.

The next day, I examined it again. I was shocked. My butt was black and blue with bruises. I almost felt guilty like I had let myself be abused or something. But I couldn't stop looking at the marks and running my fingers across my bare skin. It not only hurt to sit, but I could feel the pain each time I pulled my pants on and off. It was such a lasting sensation and that made the experience all the more powerful. I even thought about riding back out to his property to get another one, but the one thing that kept me from doing so was the markings. I don't know why but I thought it was only proper to wait until they were gone and my ass looked clean or something. I know that doesn't make sense but that's what I thought. They didn't heal in time, though, so I never made it back. The markings and pain were still there when I sat down in the seat of the plane on my way back to New York.

Q: How long ago was this?

Arianna: Last year. I am supposed to go on a trip with a couple of friends to Europe this summer but I haven't committed to it yet. I talked to my parents and asked them if that strange man still lived next to them. They said he did and wanted to know why I was asking. I'm still undecided if I'm going to go back to Australia this summer instead. It will be winter there. Not that that matters. I fantasize about the spanking nearly every week. It was so intense but I wonder if it was just the serendipity of the situation or something that got unleashed inside of me. I guess time will tell.

Naomi A., *Great Falls, Virginia*

Q: So tell me about your spanking experience.

Naomi: So the usual vibrant connection that I have with my husband had fallen into a terribly dull lull in our relationship. The daily drain of work and the grind of life had taken its toll on our energies both in and out of the bedroom. We had each been commuting in and out of D.C. and we were in desperate need of a break from politics. On a whim, we decided to throw a spontaneous cocktail party. We not only wanted to reconnect with old friends but we also craved to resuscitate the memories of living in a more reckless manner like we had done in our youthful days. We were hoping just to start out by livening up our social lives and take it from there, but neither one of us ever expected it to get so wildly livened up in the way that it was.

Q: What do you mean?

Naomi: First off, we tried to invite a wider circle of friends than we typically associate with so we could see how other couples might keep their love lives and personal lives interesting and thrilling as time passed. So we ended up with a very motley mixture of people who we both knew very well and didn't know at all. The party was going quite well but there was nothing particularly illuminating that anyone told me about their lives. That was when I started chatting with this rather unique guy who was some friend of a friend of a friend. He told me he was a writer but he was built like a lean warrior and I couldn't really pin him down at all. He spoke in thick metaphors like a poet but he didn't act like how I would expect a writer to act at all.

Q: What do you mean?

Naomi: He started touching and pawing me from the very first moment like some kind of uncivilized brute. Every writer I've met in my life is always so cerebral and will try to seduce women with his wit and intelligence. This guy would make some brilliant cutting comment and then proceed to touch me as I responded. At first, it was just a casual hand on the small of my back but then he would casually press his leg against mine and run his fingers up the back of my thigh. It was so disorienting and I should have told him to stop but I didn't. I just took a bigger swig from my wine glass and glanced over at my husband who had noticed what was happening.

Q: And how did he react to it?

Naomi: He was as unsettled as I was but he didn't seem outright upset. I could tell he was getting uncomfortably jealous, but at the same time, he smiled at me and shrugged as if to say he didn't know what to make of the guy either. We had occasionally talked about having threesomes of some sort but it never got past vague fantasies. I really had no idea what he was thinking watching all this.

Q: So what happened?

Naomi: So the guy kept up with his overt fondling of me. We were situated at the far end of the kitchen, just behind the large built-in island, so his movements were kind of hidden. The strangest thing was that he kept conversing with me as if we were having a totally normal conversation, but his hand had ascended up beneath my dress and he was carelessly groping my bare ass. He was looking straight at me the whole time with this knowing, cocksure look on his face. I can't lie. The feeling of being felt up like that and his audacity to do it openly in front of my husband was really turning me on. I was having difficulty just maintaining the discussion which I think only amused him more. Then he started tapping my bare butt cheek with the ends of his fingers.

Q: Tapping?

Naomi: Yes, just lighting tapping them against my ass – enough to make it jiggle ever so slightly. He knew that I was enjoying the attention and wasn't doing much of anything to resist him. He had his pelvis pressed up against my leg as if it was completely normal. It was then, in the middle of some random discussion, that he leaned over and bluntly told me: "You know eventually you're going to be taking this cock and there's absolutely nothing your husband can do about it?"

I was thunderstruck. No one had ever said anything like that to me in my whole life. I didn't even know how to react. I laughed in disbelief and raised my eyebrows at him. I dismissively asked him: "Really?" Yet, all he did was nod slowly up and down. Then he leaned over again and tells me: "I'm going to beat that ass bright red and dick you down so, so hard." If I hadn't been half-drunk I think I would have slapped him across his face.

Q: But you didn't reject his advances at all?

Naomi: I didn't have a chance to do anything. He gave my ass a quick slap and told me he needed to use the restroom. I was still standing there in shock as he strode away. But to top that off, on the way out of the room, he stopped to talk with my husband. I was just standing there with my mouth open as he went up to him, shook his hand and exchanged a few words with him. I watched as my husband casually smiled before this guy went off to use the restroom.

Q: So what did he tell him?

Naomi: That's what I wanted to know. I swiftly motioned for him to come over to me and I asked him what the guy told him. My husband replied that he told him that he didn't want to come across as disrespectful but that he had a magnificent wife and that she said that she wanted to have a word with him.

Q: That you wanted to have a word with your husband?

Naomi: Yes. So my husband asked me what I wanted to have a word about. This guy was really something. So I told my husband pretty much everything that he had whispered to me and how much he had been fondling me the entire time we were talking. He was obviously as stunned as I was, but the first thing he said to me was that it didn't look like I was resisting any of his overtures from where he was standing. I insisted that he caught me off-guard but he point-blank asked me if I was turned on by all of it. I had to confess to him that I was, but then he wanted to know how turned on. I asked him if he really wanted me to be honest with him and he said of course. So I told him the truth. My panties were completely soaked.

Q: So what did your husband say or do?

Naomi: He guffawed in disbelief and shook his head. He said I was acting like a little slut. I asked him if he wanted me to just tell the guy to fuck off and he thought about everything for a moment. I could tell he was really jealous but there was something more to it than that. He asked me again exactly what the guy had said to me and I told him again. He was really stirred up. He thought about it some more and then out of nowhere he told me to take off my underwear. I asked him if he was serious and he just ordered me a second time to do it. I glanced over at the house full of guests. I had nearly forgotten at this point why we were even having the party. I discreetly slipped into our walk-in pantry, closed the door and pulled them off. When I went back out and handed them to him, it became plainly obvious to him that I had absolutely no control over my sudden arousal. He repeated to me again: "You little slut."

I protested that he said he wanted to live more recklessly and that's why we were having the party. He responded that this was not exactly what he expected. Neither one of us said anything for a moment while I watched him ponder the whole thing. Finally, I asked him if he wanted me to keep talking to the guy. He said he wasn't sure. Then I asked him if he was turned on at all by it. He admitted that he was but that it all felt so out of control that he wasn't so easily enjoying it. I asked him once more what he wanted me to do and he finally just burst out: "Just don't let yourself get out of my sight! If I tell you to stop, then you stop. Is that clear?"

I told him it was crystal clear and then pulled myself toward him. I reminded him that I would never do anything behind his back. He glared at me and gave me a restrained grin. Then I whispered to him: "Baby, I'm only your little slut." I could feel him getting slightly aroused. We were getting so caught up in all of this that we had nearly forgotten about all our other guests.

Naomi: So, after about ten minutes of waiting for him to return, I went to go check on him. When I got to the guest restroom, someone was coming out of it and someone else was going in, but he wasn't anywhere around. I looked throughout the house for him but he seemed to have disappeared. I wondered for a moment if he had actually gone upstairs to use the restroom. I swiftly dashed up the stairs but there didn't seem to be anyone up there. Then, by chance, I went to check in our bedroom. I didn't really think he would have the audacity to go in there, but low and behold, the door had been opened and I could hear someone in the restroom. A few seconds later, he came strutting out as he finished pulling up the zipper on his pants.

I demanded to know what the hell he was doing in my bedroom. For a moment, I was paranoid that he had been going through my things in our bedroom. He just looked at me and grinned. He apologized and told me that the wait downstairs was too long. I was still chastising him for invading our privacy as he walked straight up to me and slipped his hand around my back. I half-heartedly pushed my hands against his chest but he simply took a hold of me by the back of my hair with his other hand and pressed his mouth to mine. I felt like I had no real will to resist his aggressive advances and it only took a few seconds for me to openly relent. His tongue was swirling deep in my mouth when he began to slide his hands under my dress.

He abruptly stopped mid-kiss and with a devious smirk asked me: "What happened to your panties?" I really wasn't sure what to say and he asked me again. I told him that my husband had asked me to take them off. This only made him more curious and he started to interrogate me about the conversation I had just had with him. I was very explicit about all of it, even telling the guy that he had called me a little slut for letting him grope me like that.

This really set him off. Without the slightest warning, he suddenly pushed me over the end of the bed, pulled up my dress and started to furiously spank me. I tried to squirm away but he held me down firmly with his arm and swatted my bare ass really hard over and over. He kept telling me that he was going to show my husband how he handled such a naughty little slut. I pleaded with him to stop and told him that we needed to go back downstairs, but he didn't seem to care what I said. For a moment, I was seriously afraid that this whole thing was getting terribly out of control. I had never been spanked so hard in my life. I was terrified that someone was going to hear or walk in, but he just kept slapping every inch of my butt over and over and over.

Q: Did you ever consider screaming or yelling for help?

Naomi: The thought did cross my mind, but I really didn't want anyone to know any of this was happening at all. Just as I was at the point where I didn't think I could take anymore, though, he stopped and let me up. He still had the same devious smirk on his face. I was just trying to gather my composure while I was berating him for spanking me so forcefully. I went to the mirror and was mortified when I saw just how reddened my ass actually was. I glared at him in disbelief, but he simply told me: "Now go show your husband what happens when his naughty wifey gets caught without her panties on."

My mind was reeling. I considered telling him he needed to just leave but I didn't. I glanced again at my crimson-colored cheeks and demanded to know why he had needed to do it so hard. He pointed to the door and repeated his order: "Go. Now." I felt like some bad little girl as I turned and walked out in a fit of anger and confusion.

He followed behind me as I trotted back downstairs to find my husband. I had no idea how he was going to react. I turned to tell the guy to wait where he was but he had already ventured off to the bar and was pouring himself another drink.

Q: So what did you tell your husband?

Naomi: I told him exactly what happened. He was just as stunned and immediately insisted on seeing for himself. We slipped into the pantry, closed the door and turned on the light. When I pulled up the back of my dress and showed him, his mouth dropped open. He questioned me over and over about every last detail. He wanted to know exactly everything that happened. It was as if he wanted to make sure nothing truly terrible had occurred while at the same time relishing every bit of information. He asked me if he had struck me anywhere else and I told him of course not. When he heard me say that he was relieved but he scolded me for letting myself get out of his sight right after he had told me not to. I insisted I didn't even have the slightest chance to tell him to come back downstairs but my husband didn't really believe me.

He leaned back on the wall and crossed his arms in frustration. He ordered me to pull up my dress and show him again, so I did. Then he said to me: "It looks like he gave you exactly what you deserved." I was astonished. I had never expected him to react like that. I pleaded with him that I hadn't done anything and that he had forced himself on me before I could get him out of our bedroom. He asked me: "So you didn't kiss him back?" I reluctantly confessed that I did. He wanted to know how exactly and I told him every last detail, even admitting to the fact that I had my tongue deep in his mouth.

"So you got what you deserved?" he repeated. I was completely exasperated. I didn't respond and he asked me once again. I finally told him that if he thought I deserved to get spanked like that then I guess I did. He was really starting to get stirred up by the entire thing. He turned me back around and pulled up my dress one last time. He ogled my reddened but for a moment and then gave it a hard smack. He added a few more on each side and then let my dress fall back down.

"I want you to go thank him for spanking your slutty little ass," he abruptly told me. I just stared at him and asked if he was serious. He said that he was absolutely serious. He told me: "You obviously have a dirty side to you that I never knew about."

I was dismayed. I pleaded with him, telling him: "Honey, are you seriously angry with me? I'll tell him to leave right now if that's what you want." He asked me if that's what I really wanted. I reiterated the fact that I was only doing this because he said it turned him on and he wanted to watch. Then he asked me point blank if "my naughty little pussy" was still wet. I tried to tell him that it didn't matter and that I would only do what he wanted me to do, but he repeated his question and ordered me to give him a yes or a no. There was no way I could lie about how my body was reacting to all of this, so I confessed that it was.

He told me: "Then get your slutty ass back out there and do what you're told." I asked him what exactly he was telling me to do and he said: "You thank him for spanking you and then you keep showing me how much you like not resisting him at all."

I looked him in the eye and confirmed with him that that was really what he wanted me to do. Yes said that it was and I told him: "Fine. Then that's what I will do." I opened the door back up and went back out.

Q: Were you thinking that this whole thing had genuinely upset your marriage?

Naomi: Yes, completely, but he was dead set on me carrying on with it. At this point, I was feeling like a slut but at the same time upset that he had completely encouraged me from the very beginning to act like that. In retrospect, I felt as if I had somehow betrayed him for allowing the guy to fondle me when we first started talking. I couldn't honestly say I didn't let him. I did. So in a weird way, I started believing that I did deserve to be punished for it. It was all so confusing. We also both had too much to drink which just amplified our emotions and actions.

Q: So how did it all play out?

Naomi: So I went back out and immediately found the guy. He was calmly waiting for me at the bar in our living room. I straight out said to him in a very formal way: "I just wanted to thank you for spanking me. My husband agreed that I was acting like a little slut and deserved it." The words sounded so strange when they came out of my mouth. He just chuckled in wry amusement. He inquired about everything that had transpired after I showed my husband what he had done and I told him. I felt like I was irredeemably caught between both of their desires and just wanted to utterly submit to being the slut they both imagined me to be.

He wanted to know if I understood now when he had told me earlier that there was nothing my husband could do about him having his way with me. I replied that I did. He eyed me for a few moments while he pondered my change of attitude. He took a sip of his drink and glanced over my shoulder at my husband. I knew he must be watching everything. He moved his hand down slyly to my bare leg and ran his fingers delicately across the inside part of my thigh. It sent shivers through me. I could feel the goosebumps form on my arms. He leaned over and whispered into my ear: "Motion for your husband to come over here." I asked him why. He said because he told me to, and so I did.

When my husband walked up, I thought I was going to lose it. The escalation of tension was unreal. The guy, though, didn't waver a single bit in his cocksure stance. He kept running his fingers up and down my thigh as he spoke with my husband.

He said to him: "So what did you think? Was the spanking sufficient or do you think she really needs her butt beaten raw?"

I cautiously glanced at my husband. I watched his eyes race from side to side, and then he took a quick sip of his cocktail. He looked back at me and our eyes met.

He replied: "I think she just might need her butt beaten raw. It seems like she has no control over that wet little cunt of hers."

I had never heard such words come out of my husband's mouth. I had butterflies.

"I think you're right," the guy said. "Has she always been such a slut?"

My husband glared at me and then said: "Maybe. I don't know. What do you think?"

It was utterly surreal to be talked about like the way they talked about me.

The guy replied: "Well, the only way you ever know with a woman is to watch her get dicked down hard and see if she has that look in her eye. Then you'll know exactly how to handle her."

"How to handle her?" asked my husband.

"Yes," the guy said. "You'll know if she can't help it. You'll know if you need to spank her hard all the time just for having the kind of cunt that says yes when her mind says no."

The words coming out of this guy just had no end in their extreme tilt. My husband leered at me. I wanted to plead my innocence but I didn't say a word.

"What exactly do you mean by dicked down hard?" my husband asked him.

The guy glanced at me and then discreetly ran his hand up my dress until it rested on my bare butt.

He told him in no uncertain terms: "Fucked. Like a dog. Head down and ass up. With size. And force." I watched my husband take another quick sip of his drink. "Is that something you'd like to see? To know if she really does deserve the kind of butt beating I gave her."

I was as shocked by his words as I was by my husband's quick response.

"Yes, that's something I'd like to see. In fact, I want to see it right now," he told him. "Let's go," he added, motioning both of us toward the stairs.

Just as we made our way, an old friend of mine approached me, telling me something about how long it had been since she had seen me. For a split second, I was brought back to the reality of this party we were throwing. It didn't matter though. I told her it was good to see her and that I would be right back.

Q: So you went through with it?

Naomi: Yes. Or to be more precise, I was taken through it. Even though it was only this one night, it lasts to this day in my mind. It forever changed the dynamic with my husband. I was never the same woman to him after he watched what he did to me.

Q: What did he do to you exactly?

Naomi: Exactly what he said he was going to do. He stripped off my dress and put me on the bed with my hands behind my back, my butt arched toward him and my eyes locked on my husband as he sat in his favorite armchair. There was nothing I could really do to conceal how good it felt. The guy knew how to speak in such a dirty and provocative manner to trigger my kinky senses in a thousand and one ways. The fact that he was well endowed and primed me with his fingers to take his full length and girth transfixed my husband. By the time he was pounding in and out of me and swatting my ass in heavy bursts, I was moaning uncontrollably. He kept telling me over and over to look at my husband. It was that good. I had to be forced to look up at him and when I saw his fierce gaze, he knew I couldn't deny what was happening. It made me crave to just unabashedly show him how good it felt to get senselessly fucked like that. By the end of it, I was shaking in orgasmic fits.

Q: And after it was all over, how were things with your husband?

Naomi: Changed irrevocably. At first, our relationship was in disarray and we had a lot of heavy talks. But in the end, we love each other just as much as before all of this. The craziest part about it is that I am really the same woman as I was when we first met, but he thinks I am now an entirely different creature. It's just that I'm older now and am open to exploring my sexuality in ways that I wasn't when we began our relationship. And so is he. I wasn't looking for wild kinky trysts with men. I was looking for love and to be loved and a husband that grows with me in every way. And I found that. Yet, he believes he's discovered this fathomless slutty side to me that was always there. In the end, it doesn't matter. Our marriage is fundamentally the same. Only now, I am thoroughly spanked practically every week, or at least every time he suspects that I am acting like a naughty little slut. I do whatever he tells me to do with other men and love when he makes me pay for it with a hard whipping and a ferocious fuck to reclaim me.

Q: So did you see this guy again?

Naomi: Nope. I never even found out his name.

Abagail W., *Cherry Hill, NJ*

Q: So tell me about your experiences getting spanked.

Abagail: My parents divorced bitterly when I was young and I grew up navigating a two-household situation. My father, though, was heavily preoccupied with his job and I rarely saw him. I didn't blame him as my mother was angry over the separation and he had to pay a tidy sum every month in alimony. Growing up, my mother was very encouraging in everything I did but it was a generic sort of optimism. She always told me I could do anything and be anybody, but almost everyone eventually discovers that that's a big lie made up by the tellers to feel good about themselves.

She went through some terrible relationships but when I was in college she finally met someone and married him. It's strange to have your mother meet, get to know and marry someone else without hardly even seeing the person. It was like waking up one day and having a new father of sorts straight from the factory. My only interactions with him were during the occasional weekend visits, but those were mostly limited to communal dinner-time chats.

In retrospect, I might have put some emotional distance between the two of us. It was not only very awkward for me to suddenly have a stepfather, but I was taken aback by the type of man that my mother ended up marrying. He worked on Wall Street and was highly ambitious. He was overbearing and would completely take over their conversations like he was in charge of her and everything around her. It was unsettling to me. She is an idealistic hippie sort of woman and always very spiritual in a touchy-

71

feely way. I would have never imagined her choosing such a man to be with for the rest of her life.

Q: So what was it like between you and him?

Abagail: Between me and Thomas? I'm not going to lie. There was an immediate strangeness. I think that even if he hadn't married my mother, there would have been an uncomfortable attraction between the two of us. I certainly had some major daddy issues, but a situation like this had never surfaced up to this point. I was profoundly uncertain of myself whenever I was around him. It was like I either wanted to just turn away from him or throw myself at him. It's hard to explain. He also has a physically very imposing presence. He is well over six feet tall and has thick black hair that is always groomed to perfection. It made me feel like just a little girl around him.

We had limited interactions while I was away at college, but after I graduated, I moved to the city to pursue a career as a dancer. I had trained in ballet since I was four and it was my always dream to perform in a major ballet in New York City. When the recession hit, though, I was struggling just to pay my bills with three different part-time jobs. I hardly had enough time to train, much less be at the level to land a part with a top dance company. I told my mother that I was thinking about moving back home but she didn't feel like that was a very good idea. She told me she would talk to Thomas. I assumed that she meant that she was going to talk to him about me moving back which made me feel really awkward. It was like I needed a stranger's permission to return to my own home.

The next day, though, my mother told me that Thomas wanted to meet with me. I immediately asked her why and she told me that he wanted to discuss my dancing career. We quickly began to argue as I didn't think it was any of his business. My mother pleaded with me to just meet with him to hear him out and I relented.

Q: How did the meeting go?

Abigail: I was supposed to meet him in the evening after one of my dance classes, but he showed up at the studio in the middle of the class. I was totally caught off-guard. There is this little viewing window on the side of the dance studio that lets people look in without disturbing the class. I was working with the teacher, repeating this one move over and over, and I suddenly looked over to see his face in the window. I don't know why but it completely threw me off. He rested his arms on the edge of the window and started to watch me in this really intense way. It was like he was studying my performance and I was on trial. I felt so self-conscious. I mean I am used to people watching me dance but it is normally a crowd of strangers or a group of friends. Knowing that he was watching me like that made me feel so vulnerable. It was as if I was half-naked in front of him and couldn't do anything about it.

Anyway, after practice ended, we went to a café next door to talk. I had assumed that we were going to discuss my moving in with him and my mother, but he immediately asked me about my future plans for ballet. I tried to explain it to him the best I could but he simply stared back at me with a quizzical look on his face. Then, he told me that he didn't know anything about ballet but he believed that most young women who pursued it just had wistful dreams that didn't mesh with reality. I immediately protested, telling him that there have been successful ballerinas for hundreds of years. He asked me bluntly if I truly believed that I was one of those elite few. I had never been asked that question in such black-and-white terms. I could feel the blood boiling inside me over his sudden intrusion into my life. I knew that I not only had to give him an honest answer, I suddenly had to be honest with myself.

Q: How did you respond?

Abigail: I'm not going to lie. I had doubts, but it wasn't in me to back down. I mustered every ounce of confidence and told him that I was absolutely one of those elite few. He stared directly into my eyes as I spoke as if he was studying the veracity of my resolve. He told me that he understood that there are ballerinas who are successful both artistically and financially, but that he was sure it demanded extreme discipline. He asked me if I was ready for that. I told him that I was.

He nodded up and down while he seemed to be contemplating everything. Then he explained to me that he was a businessman and that's what he knew. He understood that you can't get any business off the ground without capital. I wasn't sure why he was even telling me all of this. There was a strange moment of silence and then he made his proposal to me.

Q: His proposal?

Abigail: Yes. He told me that he would fully finance my career for two years but that he had to be assured that I was being completely disciplined and making genuine progress. I was totally stunned. It was the last thing I expected him to tell me and I didn't how to respond. The idea of having complete freedom to pursue dancing was like a dream come true for me, but the fact that I would suddenly have no excuses for why I couldn't make it terrified me. It's kind of like that phrase, "Be careful what you ask for because you just might get it." I was afraid to immediately agree to his proposal. I asked him how he would judge my progress. He told me that he would speak directly with my teacher to determine if I was making the necessary advancement. The idea that he would be holding me accountable like that felt very strange and intrusive, but at the same time, there was something incredibly alluring about it. It felt comforting in a way I had never experienced.

I asked him then what would happen if he thought I wasn't making progress. He told me that we would cross that bridge when we came to it. The most important thing, he said, is that I always stay disciplined. He asked me if I understood and I said that I did.

Q: So that was it? So how did the agreement work out?

Abigail: At the beginning, it was fantastic. Without the stress of having to work three jobs and practice dance at the same time, my form improved dramatically. Thomas would stop by the dance studio from time to time and watch me. At first, it made me hyper self-conscious but I slowly began to enjoy his presence there. It was reassuring. Not only was I ecstatic about how good I was getting, but I got the sense that I was pleasing him in some way. Some evenings he would drive me back to my apartment before he headed home and we would talk about various things. Sometimes we would talk about dancing but other times we would talk about movies or politics or whatever. We grew very comfortable with one another.

But then one day, everything changed. He met with my teacher and she told him that I was a very good dancer but that I wasn't anywhere close to the caliber of where I needed to be to make a career out of it. She told him that I needed to push myself a lot harder if I was going to get anywhere at all. I was absolutely devastated when he told me what she said.

Q: How did he react?

Abigail: At first, he didn't say anything. He was driving me home and I was sulking the whole time about what my teacher had said. I really thought I was slowly growing to be a great dancer but I guess I had been deluding myself about how much progress I had actually made. I started to cry. I asked Thomas if this meant he was going to stop supporting me. He glared over at me as he was driving and then abruptly pulled the car to the side of the road. He started shouting at me, telling me: "Don't you dare question yourself. Is this how you were taught to react to adversity?" He was really sincerely upset with me and then I became angry with myself for reacting the way I did.

I told him, "Okay, okay. You're right. I'll try harder." He sensed right away, though, that they were just hopeful-sounding words coming out of my mouth. I wasn't really confident that it was just a matter of me pushing myself. I had seriously begun to doubt that I had the natural ability to make it at all. When we pulled up outside my apartment, I was still wiping the tears from my eyes. When he looked at me and saw that I was still acting like I was feeling sorry for myself, it triggered something inside of him.

He started hollering at me. He asked me: "What did I tell you about staying disciplined? You made the choice to pursue this career. This is an adult world you're living in now. If you're going to cry like a little girl, I'm going to spank your little butt like one. Is that clear?"

I couldn't believe it when he threatened me with a spanking. I didn't know how to react. He spoke to me like some strict father who was disappointed with his daughter. It was so disorienting. I tried to tell him how difficult it all was but he wasn't having any part of it.

Q: What happened?

Abigail: He suddenly shoved the gear shift into park and turned on the hazard lights. He said to me: "Get out. I'm going to give you something to cry about." A torrent of fear washed over me. I had no idea what he meant or what he planned to do, but he had already gotten out of the car and was halfway around the front of it. I opened my door and he just grabbed me firmly by the arm. I protested, asking him what he was doing but he didn't respond. I never had someone grab me like that.

He slammed the door shut and ushered me up the front steps of my apartment building. I was totally afraid but I didn't really know what to say to him. I had this weird sensation of having been caught acting naughty but I didn't really know what I was feeling because he was so intimidating and was being so forceful with me. My hands were shaking when I took out my keys to open the front door. He still had his hand securely around my arm and he led me inside. It seemed like we were down the hall and inside of my apartment in a matter of seconds. It all happened in a dramatic rush.

He took a quick look around my place and then grabbed a chair from this little table I had next to the kitchen. He turned the back of it around and practically slammed it down on the floor in front of me. He shouted at me to bend over it. He was already undoing his belt. I was so startled and didn't really know what was happening. I had never even been spanked before and the sight of his belt was terrifying. I was so overwhelmed by his outburst that I couldn't fully process what was happening. I froze in place for a moment and just watched him take his belt out of the loops of his pants. He folded it in half and gave me a stern look. He said to me again: "Bend over the chair, Abbie. You're going to get a good hard spanking and a lesson about the consequences of having a bad attitude."

Q: And what did you do?

Abigail: When he said the word "spanking", all these weird images went through my mind. I thought about all these kinky scenes from movies and old photos. I was speechless. I wondered if my mother knew he was going to do this or if this was something happening just between the two of us. I wanted to placate him in whatever way he wanted and get it over with, but submitting to a belt whipping for not an easy thing to do. I briefly glanced at him as he waited and then reluctantly bent over the back of the metal chair. I rested my hands on the cold metal seat. I instantly felt so vulnerable and exposed. I was still wearing my dance pants and I could feel them stretch tautly around my butt.

He didn't give me any time to react, though. He began to scold me right away, telling me that he was going to teach me "how to take what life dishes out." When the first stroke of his leather belt whipped across my cheeks, my body jolted forward. I cried out in shock and pleaded to him to please be easy on me as I had never been spanked. He replied that I was going to take what I had earned and learn how to react to the pain of adversity. He whipped it across my butt a few more times as I twisted and turned to absorb the pain.

Q: Did you feel at all like he was crossing a line he shouldn't cross by physically disciplining you?

Abigail: Kind of. I mean the whole situation felt very taboo in many ways. But, I could have gotten up and run out of there if I really wanted to and I didn't. There was something about being in his presence that made me feel like I wanted to submit to his authority just to see what an older man like him would do to me. It sounds a bit perverse, I know, but I was still young and so inexperienced. Underneath my feelings of fear, the whole time was this insatiable craving to be taught how to make it through this difficult time in my life.

Q: So what happened next?

Abigail: He paused for a moment and asked me: "Do you feel how badly that stings?" I readily replied that I did. Then he started to lecture me. He said: "That is the sting of defeat, Abbie. If you want to be successful in ballet, or in anything, you need to learn that it is all a matter of how instinctively you bounce back from defeat. You need to eagerly strive to overcome adversity the moment it strikes you. Do you understand?"

His corny sermon was oddly reassuring and somehow revelatory in a very uncomfortable way. I pondered for a moment if such teachings were what fathers typically did with their daughters and if I had missed out on it all. I told him that I understood, but I was really just beginning to understand his forceful lesson.

He said to me: "Abbie, you're going to get as many strokes of this belt as you think you need in order to move forward. Is that clear?"

I was baffled. It wasn't clear at all to me and I told him I didn't understand. He calmly explained that it was my responsibility to welcome the sting of life's setbacks and to persevere. I was still perplexed and asked him if he could just show me what he wanted out of me.

He said that he would make it unforgettably clear. He reared back with his belt and whipped it across my sore cheeks once again. Then he spontaneously told me: "Say thank you, Daddy." His words absolutely floored me. A wave of shivers fluttered through me. He quickly spanked me again and told me once more to say it.

I bashfully mumbled the words to him: "Thank you, Daddy." For a moment, I was almost angry that he was making me call him Daddy but he didn't even give me a chance to protest. He swiftly whipped the belt across my butt once again and I flinched from the pain.

And then he told me: "Say thank you, Daddy. May I have another?"

I took a deep breath, but I reluctantly complied and told him: "Thank you, daddy. May I have another?"

He spanked me with the belt once more and asked me to repeat the same mantra. He proceeded to soundly whip it across my tender cheeks again and again, each time waiting for me to tell him thank you and ask for another. I would flinch with each stroke of the belt, but after another half dozen of them, I began to grow more accustomed to the sensation. It suddenly occurred to me like some epiphany that this was what he meant when he said I would get as many strokes as I thought I needed. He was letting me know that I was in charge of overcoming the pain and he was merely playing the daddy role in my need for guidance. It was so oddly ingenious and once that fact became clear, the spanking took on a whole different intensity.

Q: How so?

Abigail: I wanted to prove to myself that I could take being spanked as hard as he wanted to spank me. I wanted to show him that each strike of his belt only made me stronger and more resolute. So, after the next time he whipped it across my butt, I held my body firm and ignored the pain. The tone of my voice swiftly turned more assertive. It was as if I was suddenly telling him I wanted another one rather than asking for one. After a handful more, I defiantly stated in a raised voice: "Thank you, Daddy. I would like another."

When he heard my abrupt change of demeanor and the firm stance of my body, he commenced to spank me even harder. As each whip of his belt lashed heavier and heavier across my ass, the more determined I became to take anything he could dish out. When he paused to rest for a moment, I turned my head back and told him: "I said I would like another."

He nodded in a kind of shared understanding and a look of approval spread across his face. He gave me probably a dozen more strokes, each one harder than the last. At some point, the thin fabric of my dance pants had torn and I could feel the slick leather strike my bare skin. No matter how much it hurt, though, I took it as if it didn't affect me in the least. He finally stopped and told me that he thought that was enough. I stood up and twisted around to take a look at my back side. The leggings were torn like a pair of cheap nylons and I could see the vivid red stripes on my naked cheeks. I was suddenly a bit embarrassed when the reality of me standing there so exposed became apparent. I was so caught up in my emotions, though, that it didn't really matter. He reached over to me and gave me a warm hug, telling me that I was a good girl. Without even thinking I said: "Thank you, daddy." When he glanced up at me, I must have been totally blushing.

Q: That all must have been quite dramatic.

Abigail: To say the least. After he left, I replayed the whole scenario back through my mind and it finally hit me just how crazy and taboo it all was. The first thing I asked myself was if he was going to mention any of this to my mother. I assumed that this was something completely between the two of us, but it now occurred to me how outrageous the situation truly was. I mean I was 23 years old and my stepfather who I was just barely getting to know had just giving me a very harsh spanking with his belt. Not only could I not tell my mother, but I couldn't possibly tell anyone about this.

Q: So life just went on as normal afterward?

Abigail: Yes and no. The next day, my stepfather texted me to let me know that he had told my mother that we had a serious "talk" and that she was happy I was so determined to make it as a dancer. I was relieved and I took it to mean that this spanking thing was solely between me and him. In any case, I was completely reinvigorated. I worked my ass off like never before and became unbelievably competitive. Any expression of dissatisfaction or discouragement from my ballet teacher I shrugged off or took as a challenge to push myself even harder.

Q: So did the spanking actually serve its purpose?

Abigail: It did for a while, but I still felt terribly alone in my pursuits and it was so difficult to go at it like that day-in and day-out. I really didn't have anyone else who was there for me expect from my family. I started to get a bit burnt out and I wanted to tell my stepfather but I couldn't bring myself to it.

Q: What do you mean?

Abigail: I couldn't stop thinking about him spanking me and about me calling him Daddy. There was a part of me that totally wanted that kind of relationship with him all the time, but then I would wake up to the reality that this man was married to my mother and I was a grown ass adult. To confess that I really needed it made me angry at myself and I'd just block it out of my mind and carry on.

Q: So what did you do?

Abigail: I texted him one night and asked him if he was free. He called me and asked what was wrong. I just blurted out: "Daddy, I need another spanking." I felt like such a freak but I was really so exhausted. To my relief, he told me he understood and that he would stop by later to talk with me.

Q: To talk with you?

Abigail: Yes. I mean we did have a heavy conversation when he came over but it was really just a prelude to another spanking session. This one didn't last as long as the first one but it gave me what I needed. There's nothing like the dopamine rush from getting a hard spanking and the lingering sensation that lasts for days. Plus, there was something entirely comforting about the ritual of calling him Daddy and asking for a spanking. In a perverse way, I felt loved in this strangely innocent way. Afterward, he told me that he was proud of me for all the progress I was making but I should set aside days just to rest and not think about ballet at all. He insisted I create more balance in my life as he wouldn't be happy if I ended up getting hurt or quitting because it became unfulfilling. He told me that from now on I would have a strict set schedule that I would have to abide by.

Q: A schedule?

Abigail: Yes. Days and times when I would be practicing ballet, days and times when I needed to rest, and even days and times that I would be spanked. He even gave me a strict bedtime curfew so I would get plenty of rest. I know it might sound crazy but I really needed someone to give me firm guidelines like that. If it wasn't for that fact that he started spanking me nearly every week, the whole situation wouldn't have been so preposterous and taboo. But I probably craved the ritualistic spankings more than any of it. The physicality of it gave me this cathartic release and rejuvenated me for the week.

Q: And it was always the same ritual?

Abigail: No, sometimes he would just put me over his lap and spank me with his hand. And after the first few times, he began to always swat me on my bare ass. That really made it feel so deviant and forbidden. There was though always a certain ritual to it. We always talked about my issues with ballet or something else that was going on in my personal life, and then he would tell me in a very formal manner to get the chair or to get over his lap. There was always a bit of scolding and him making me tell him why I had earned a spanking. It was this weird routine that I craved more than anything. I wish it could have gone on longer.

Q: What happened that made it stop?

Abigail: I ended up meeting someone who I started seriously dating. I would have been horrified if he had found out about it. Plus, I hated feeling so guilty that I was having this unusual relationship with my stepfather and my mother didn't know about any of it. I had a long talk with him one day and we decided it would be best just to end the spanking sessions.

Q: And the ballet?

Abigail: No, I would never quit that unless my body gave out. I finally made it onto a company. It wasn't the American Ballet Theater or anything that prestigious, but I'm totally happy where I am at with things. Plus, I have slowly got my boyfriend into spanking so now I have that to look forward to. I really can't complain how life has turned out so far.

Adrienne L., *Kansas City, MO*

Q: Tell me about your experiences getting spanked.

Adrienne: I was visiting my daughter in New York where she goes to school. She had a new boyfriend and I invited him out with us to this fancy French restaurant. I was a bit shocked when I met him. My daughter usually dates more sensitive types, like musicians or the young intellectual kind of guy. This guy was very intense and masculine with this really commanding presence. He was well-built like a baseball player and he was studying pre-law. He had these dark brown eyes that just locked onto me the moment I shook his hand. He insisted on getting a town car instead of a taxi and opened the door for me and my daughter to get in like a gentleman.

When we got to the restaurant and started talking, I was taken aback by how well-read he was and how forceful and developed he was in how he spoke. I had grown up with very manly men but it was the first time my daughter had actually dated one. Anyway, neither I nor my daughter liked what we ordered so we just stopped eating. In the middle of the meal, he looked over at my daughter and gave her this stern look. He told her to finish and made a remark that this wasn't a fast food restaurant and people worked hard for such expensive meals.

It took me by surprise because it was the kind of old-fashioned way of thinking that I had grown up with in the Midwest but had not instilled in my daughter. I had married wealthy and had given her everything that I never had growing up. I felt embarrassed that he was reprimanding her for not eating her food because he was right. She was spoiled and she didn't appreciate the luxury.

Q: So what happened?

Adrienne: Well, the moment he gave her that look, my daughter looked at me and then laughed self-consciously. She looked back at her boyfriend and he told her right there at the table that she better finish her dinner or she would get it when they got home. I was totally shocked and it was a really awkward moment. I just excused myself to go to the restroom, but when I came back her plate was empty. Not long after, we left and stopped for a drink at a nice bar next door. We had a couple of drinks and I was getting a little tipsy. When my daughter stepped away to use the restroom, her boyfriend looked over at me with that same stern look. You know what he said to me?

Q: What?

Adrienne: He said: "You really coddled her. She thinks she can have anything. She's going to have a tough time when people tell her no."

Q: And what did you say?

Adrienne: I was speechless. I was so angry that this young man was telling me the faults in my parenting but at the same time, I knew that there was some truth to it. I just made a casual remark that he was probably right but I just let it go. But under the surface, his words really got to me. I ordered another drink and then another. By the time we left the place, I was so drunk that I tripped on the sidewalk and nearly fell. I had to grab onto him just to keep from ending up face-first on the sidewalk. When I looked up at him, he gave me that same stern look. It sent a chill through me.

So he hailed us a couple of taxis. One for me to go back to my hotel and then another for my daughter to go back to her apartment. He opened the door for the first one and looked at my daughter to get in. I didn't know what to think. He just told her that he would see her the next day, kissed her and closed the car door. The taxi sped off before I had a chance to say anything. He turned around and glared at me with that same look as he opened the door for the other taxi for me. As I went to get inside, I nearly fell off the curb again I was so tipsy. I grabbed onto his arm for support. He told me in this really firm, angry voice: "You've had too much to drink. I'm taking you back to your hotel."

Q: What did you do?

Adrienne: I didn't do anything. He ushered me into the taxi and climbed in. We were speeding off toward my hotel before I had a chance to react. He looked over at me and guess what he said next.

Q: What?

Adrienne: He asks me: "Tell me why I shouldn't give you a good hard spanking when we get back to the hotel." I nearly lost my mind. My head was spinning from the alcohol and I was speechless. I suddenly felt like a little girl who knew that she had been caught being naughty. I began to laugh because I didn't know how else to react. It just seemed so unreal to be sitting in the back of the taxi and being threatened with a spanking. He just raised his eyebrows in response to my laughter. He was absolutely serious. I had butterflies in my stomach just looking at him. I mumbled something to him like: "You're crazy. You're not going to spank me. I'm your girlfriend's mother."

Q: And what did he say?

Adrienne: He said, "That's all the more reason. We need to set things straight now." I couldn't believe it. I think my mouth was still open in shock when we pulled up in front of the hotel. He paid the driver, opened the door, got out and then waited for me to get out. I still remember his face as he was bent over at the door of the taxi. He was wearing a white dress shirt and had rolled up the sleeves.

I inched across the back seat and when I got to the edge of the door, he grabbed me by my arm. I nearly gasped. He said: "Let's go. Now." He took me forcefully by my arm like I was a disobedient girl. I was protesting the whole time but, thinking back, I was hardly putting up a fight.

Q: What do you mean?

Adrienne: I mean that he had just cued into some part of me and deep down I was intoxicated by the whole moment. I needed him to force me across the hotel lobby and into the elevator. I don't know what I would have done if I had time to think about it rationally. At one point, I started to say something and he said: "Shut your mouth, young lady, or you'll get spanked harder." I couldn't believe it.

Q: So what happened?

Adrienne: He tugged me the whole way down the hall with his hand firmly gripped around my arm. When we got to my room, he just grabbed my purse and took out the room key card. He opened it up and ushered me inside. It all happened so fast and was so unexpected. I stumbled into the room and he didn't waste any time. He pushed me over the edge of the bed, lifted up the edge of my dress and started spanking me. His hands were strong and large, and they felt like they were striking my whole butt every time he spanked me. I struggled to move away as I called out his name asking him to stop but he just grabbed me by my waist and kept spanking me.

Q: Did he say anything?

Adrienne: Yes. He kept saying that I was acting like a spoiled brat and there would be no more uneaten dinners and drunken falls.

Q: How did you react?

Adrienne: At first, I kept calling out his name and telling him that had no right to do this. But after he really started spanking me harder and scolding me for my behavior, I began to apologize, saying "Okay, okay, there won't be." I couldn't believe I was being disciplined for it but deep down I felt he was right to do it. I had just never met anyone that had the audacity to do such a thing. Plus, I was feeling this weird guilt that my daughter's boyfriend was being physical like this with me. He was just so assertive and forceful in how he did everything.

Q: Everything?

Adrienne: Yes, well even after I apologized to him for getting drunk and not finishing my dinner, he didn't stop. In fact, he suddenly pulled my underwear down and started to spank me on my bare ass. I nearly lost my mind. I tried to turn around to stop him. I called out his name and asked him what he was doing. He tells me, "This is for coddling your daughter like a spoiled princess. There will be no more of that. Understand?" It was like this weird role reversal of everything. I felt like he was tearing down my role as a mother and making me his naughty girl.

Q: Did you like it?

Adrienne: Well, yes. Especially imagining it in the aftermath. But while it was happening, it was just confusing and intense. I didn't have time to think about it. It was all very raw and overwhelming. I mean for a couple of minutes during the spanking, I just stopped speaking and felt his hand striking my bare butt over and over. I just accepted the spanking and almost enjoyed the pain. The feeling of being in the man's arms, my daughter's boyfriend's arms, was suddenly so kinky and taboo. I felt like he was right to spank me but I was struggling more against how wrong it felt for him to assert his authority over me. I felt like I had to struggle even though I was loving every moment the palm of his hand slapped against my flesh.

Q: What happened next?

Adrienne: Eventually, I apologized enough and promised to change my behavior that he stopped and let me up. I pulled my underwear up and turned to look at him. He still had that stern look in his eyes and he looked absolutely devastating. The muscles in his forearms were constricted and he was breathing heavily. If he would have taken me right there, I don't think I could have resisted.

Q: But he didn't?

Adrienne: No, there was an undeniable attraction between the two of us. He knew I liked the spanking and I knew that he liked giving it, but we both knew we couldn't cross that line. He was very controlled like that. I've never met anyone who could be so impulsive with their actions but still restrain themselves.

Q: What did you say to each other?

Adrienne: We didn't say anything for a few moments. His shirt had come un-tucked and he went to the bathroom to straighten up his appearance. When he got back, I didn't know what to say. I really did feel like the naughty spanked girl waiting for her disciplinarian to say the right words. He looked at me and then said to me, "I hope you don't think I do this all the time. I've just had more than enough of your daughter's behavior." I told him that I understood. I don't know why I said it but I did. I wondered how often he spanked my daughter and how we were all going to react around each other after this. He just reached over and kissed me on the cheek, and then told me good night.

Q: And how were things between all of you after this?

Adrienne: Fine. I mean we all went out to dinner again a couple of nights later and it was very awkward at first. I assumed he hadn't said anything to my daughter but I wasn't completely positive. But after we sat down to eat, we all started conversing like normal. He glanced at me a couple of times as I was eating as if to remind me of things. It sent a chill through me again but there was this strange pleasure in knowing that he expected the two of us to finish our dinner. I know it sounds silly but it turned me on to eat knowing that he was watching me. Every time we ate together after that, the whole evening was so erotically charged. I even once thought about not finishing my dinner in front of him to see what he would do.

Q: Did you?

Adrienne: No. The memory of the one spanking lasted for quite a while. It changed the whole dynamic with my daughter. It was as if she knew that he had talked to me by the way I started talking to her. I believe she wanted to ask me but I think deep down she knew how he was and was afraid of the possibility that he had actually done something to me. I think she had an idea in the back of her head that he spanked me that night but there was no way I would ever confess to it.

Q: Do you want him to do it again?

Adrienne: Yes, more than anything. But they broke up a few months later. So, it's all in the past now. Just a really potent memory that comes up every time I visit her.

Marianna S., *Bronx, NY*

Q: So tell me about your experiences getting spanked.

Marianna: Well, I have pretty much gotten it for most of my life but it wasn't until I was in my mid-twenties that I really started to crave it as an integral part of a larger desire for domestic discipline in my relationships. Being on the receiving end of spankings and discipline has been a part of my existence for so long now that I can't even imagine living without it. For a while, I was very conflicted about it because of the way I grew up, but now I wholeheartedly embrace every aspect of it. I am in love with the whole routine – the anticipation, the stern looks, the lecturing, the positioning, the release, the aftercare – but especially the structure and guidance that come with it. Yet, at some point along the way, I also realized that to be truly open to being in a domestic discipline-type relationship, I need to respect the man in the larger world. I have to trust that his authority is grounded in wisdom and experience in life.

Q: So what do you mean that you have gotten it for most of your life?

Marianna: I mean I pretty much grew up getting it. My mother married my stepfather when I was 15 and he was really strict. We lived in a tough neighborhood and he felt like I needed to be very disciplined in order to avoid making the mistakes a lot of girls make as teenagers. He was Colombian and had a very patriarchal view of things. He had a flag on the wall and was very proud to have made it to the U.S. He thought he was a Scarface of his own small working world. He would walk around without his shirt off and had a tattoo of the Virgin Mary on his arm.

Q: So what ages did you get it?

Marianna: I got it well into my teens. The last one I got was when I was 19, just before I moved out.

Q: How did you deal with getting it from your stepfather at that age?

Marianna: It was mostly embarrassing that I was the only one of my friends getting it at that age. Also, there were definitely some extreme conflicts when he first moved in. I had been sporadically disciplined by both my parents before they divorced but to suddenly have a man who I wasn't related to taking over the household in such a strict fashion was a serious upheaval to everything I thought about men and women and families. For the initial few months, I tried to keep to my own space but I was naturally rebellious so confrontation was inevitable. Plus, because I was already a teenager when he moved in, there was always this weird sexual tension between the two of us. I was really confused because I told myself that he wasn't my father but at the same time he was a very tough manly guy who commanded the respect of everyone who knew him. He was uncomfortably attractive to me on another level but I had no idea what to do with those feelings. In my subconscious, I probably wished that he wanted me more than he wanted my mother. I'm a regular Freudian case study, I know.

Q: So you hated being disciplined by him but you also craved his physical attention?

Marianna: Yes, kind of. Like I said, I grew up in a rough Latino neighborhood so trying to be strong and act strict with your loved ones was the norm. He was just much stricter than my friends' fathers. The fact that he wasn't my real father, though, became very formative in how I thought of guys I dated later on. He actually hung this old-fashioned razor strap on the back of my door as a kind of reminder of what was in store for me if I didn't behave. It was double-stripped. Smooth horsehide leather on one side and thick woven nylon on the other. He would use both sides. I remember that it said "Bell Barbers Supply Company" on the top of the strap because I had to look at it every day.

Q: What did you get spanked for?

Marianna: Just about everything at one time or another. In the beginning, it was because I refused to accept him as my father and abide by his rules. Eventually, he decided to lay down the law with me and teach me to respect him to the nth degree. I got it for many, many things – talking back, bad grades, coming home past curfew, cussing, being late for school, clothes he thought were inappropriate, not finishing homework before dinner. A lot of the discipline had to do with school. He expected straight A's and anything less would result in a strapping. He didn't know anything about education but he knew it was vital to making a better life for oneself. At the end of high school, when I was 18, I went through a very rebellious stage and started getting them regularly.

Q: What is regularly?

Marianna: Well, he would sometimes put me on what he called "restriction" when I got caught ditching school and sneaking out at night to party with boys. I would not only be grounded and have many privileges taken away, but during the time I was on restriction, I would be spanked after dinner and sent to bed. I only got put on restriction maybe a half dozen times, but it was awful when I got it. Sometimes it was for a few days and sometimes it was for a week.

Q: How did he spank you exactly?

Marianna: When I was younger it was usually in my bedroom, but after I turned 18 it was always in the living room. He liked to make an example out of me and didn't really care who saw. When he told me I earned a spanking, he would order me to go into the kitchen and get one of the chairs. We had a set of metal kitchen chairs with red vinyl on the seats. I carried the chair into the living room and placed it on the center of the rug. Then I was just expected to bare myself, bend over it and wait to be disciplined. It was so humiliating. I think the neighbors even saw me sometimes from the windows across the street.

So when he finally came to spank me, he would always say: "On your toes, mi hija." I had to stand up on my tip toes the whole time and keep my back arched. It made it so I couldn't squirm away, I guess. So, he would take the strap and run it across my bare bottom so I knew I was about to get it. Then he would ask me what I did wrong and make me tell him why it was wrong. If I gave him an inadequate answer, he would immediately strap me five times and tell me to try again. He was big on making sure I gave a real reason why it was wrong to do what I did and that I thought it out for myself.

So once I gave him the right answer, he would tell me how many I was going to get for what I had done wrong. It could be anywhere from 10 to 50. He'd make me count them out after every stroke of the strap. Very formal and ritualistic. Afterward, he would hand me the strap and tell me to go hang it back in its place. I would pace back to my room, sulking and crying, and hang the strap back on the back of the door.

Q: How did you feel about getting spanked by him?

Marianna: I was really conflicted. I was young so I didn't have anything to compare it to. It was just what I knew. But I felt like I was taking the pain for the whole family. My mother and stepfather really struggled to make ends meet. They would work 12 hours some days and still barely be able to pay the bills. I felt like that if I didn't do well in school that I deserved the spankings in some way. It's a different mentality when you just want to make something out of yourself in life. At the same time, he really took it to an extreme and my mother was perfectly fine with it. I sensed that she was terrified that I would end up working myself to the bone like she did and never get anywhere. I don't know. It was just a very impressionable part of being a teenager for me.

Q: This was when you were 18?

Marianna: Yes, I got them through the end of high school and then into my first two years of college. After that, I moved out.

Q: How did you feel getting spanked at that age?

Marianna: I hated it but I had gotten used to it by then. I tried to keep it secret from all my friends because it was so embarrassing to be punished like that when you feel like you are an adult. Plus, he was my stepfather, so there was always this feeling of being dominated by another man. I think he disciplined my mother as well but I never saw anything. She was almost always there when he spanked me and she totally approved. She liked that he was the head of the household because she had difficulty with me on her own. I think it gave her a sense of control and peace of mind to see me spanked like that, especially when I was older and started dating.

Q: What do you mean?

Marianna: Well, we had a few talks about the spankings. She was the first one to tell me that I should find a man like my stepfather. I thought she was crazy. I thought I didn't want to be with a man anything like my stepfather so I would date really artsy or punk types who were the opposite of my stepfather. It displeased my mother so she would sometimes come up with little things that she thought I needed to be spanked for after I would come home on a date with one of them. It was her twisted way of disapproving.

Q: And what about after you moved out?

Marianna: Well, I was never spanked by my stepfather again, but I went through a really difficult time. I moved into an apartment with a friend and I went crazy with all the new freedom. I was not only ecstatic to be living on my own but there was no one there to motivate me or keep me from going astray. I would go out drinking and smoking weed almost every night, was hooking up with guys every chance I got and my grades fell so far that I got put on academic probation. I didn't know what to do. I saw a psychologist and we talked about how I had never learned to do things for myself, that I needed to be self-disciplined and things like that. It got better the next year, but when I graduated, the whole cycle started again. I would simply get depressed if I had to really push myself to get things done at work and eventually I got fired. I didn't know what to do. I wasn't about to move home again.

Q: So what happened?

Marianna: Well, I lived with one of my friends for a while and suddenly started dating other kinds of men.

Q: What do you mean?

Marianna: Well, I started having more and more fantasies about getting disciplined. At first, I thought it was so twisted and tried to push it out of my mind, but it began to turn me on more than anything else. So, I finally would just bring it up casually in conversation with men at bars or make a joke about it on my online dating profile. It worked very well. I went on a lot of dates with really assertive men and guys who liked to be controlling. Ironically, there was something deep down that turned me on about them being strict with me, even after all the years of thinking about nothing but getting out of my strict household forever. For a year, I was hooking up with one guy just so he would take me home and spank me for something I had done wrong at work. One time, I was drunk in a bar and really mouthing off to this guy just to get him all riled up. He ended up taking me out to the parking lot and spanking me in the back seat of his car. It slowly became the norm in my life to seek out discipline.

Q: Any serious relationships?

Marianna: Yes, that is how I met Andres, my husband.

Q: Your husband? Tell me about that.

Marianna: Well, during one of my really bad spells, I actually got arrested for drunk driving. It was a very eye-opening experience and I was in such an emotional state. Andres was the arresting officer and he was trying to calm me down and I blurted out that I just needed a good spanking. I saw that look in his eyes and we both knew there was an instant connection even beyond that. He asked me where I was from and we found out we had grown up in the same neighborhood. He even knew who my stepfather was. I told him that I couldn't afford to get arrested and begged him to let me go. Later on, he told me that the only reason he let me go was that he could never take me out if fellow officers knew he had brought me in on a charge.

Q: So he let you go?

Marianna: Yes. He told me he would deal with my discipline later on. He made me lock my car, call an Uber and text him when I got home. It was very sweet and heartfelt. We went out the next week and we completely fell for each other. He is entirely the perfect man for me in every way. I can talk to him about absolutely anything in a genuinely honest way but he also creates this world of structure and guidance for me that I profoundly crave and need in my life.

Q: So how did he deal with your discipline?

Marianna: Well, on the second date, he asked me about what I had said about needing a good spanking. I just openly confessed about how I was spanked as a teenager. He told me his father raised his sister in the same way and that he didn't see anything wrong with it. I couldn't believe it. All these years I had kept it as sort of a secret in serious relationships and he saw it as totally normal. It might sound kind of twisted but I feel like I can't exist without the threat of a spanking hanging over me.

Q: So what happened?

Marianna: He bluntly told me I was going to be soundly spanked for the drunk driving incident. I was fine with that but then he told me that he was going to do it right in front of my stepfather. He said it was the only way he could be sure I would be so humiliated that I would never drive drunk again. I was absolutely shell-shocked. I told him there was no way that that was going to happen. He told me that that was the only way it was going to happen. I didn't tell him at the time but I really salivated over the fact that he was so unrelenting in the end. I now like that sort of consensual non-consent dynamic and am fine with ultimately having no final say in how things are going to be with him.

I think, though, he also really liked the very idea of it and wanted to ritualistically take the reins from my stepfather. He has these old-fashioned notions of men sticking together and taking care of their women in very paternalistic ways. It was something I thought I really hated about some men but I was now strangely attracted to such archaic thinking. Even after my defiant objections he simply told me to invite my parents out to dinner so they could all formally meet. So we all went out and he and my stepfather totally hit it off. It was so weird to have the two significant men in your life connect like that.

Q: So what happened after that?

Marianna: So a number of months later, he told me to call my stepfather and hand him the phone. I did and he brought up my drunk driving incident. I couldn't believe it. He told my stepfather that I had told him about how I was raised and was a firm believer in discipline himself. He asked him to come over the following night to assist with my punishment. He also asked him to bring the strap I was raised with. It was all so surreal. It was like he was asking for his permission to become serious with me and wanted my stepfather to know that I would be cared for in the same strict manner.

Q: And did your stepfather agree?

Marianna: Yes, of course. When he heard that I had got pulled over for drunk driving, he was outraged, but I know that he was really happy at the same time that I had met someone like Andres. Strangely, it was a weird relief for me as well. I had grown apart from my parents after I moved out and this helped to bring the skeletons out of the closet.

Q: Did you ever question that all these spankings were physical abusive in some way?

Marianna: Not really, but for a time while I was in college and seeing a counselor, I did start heavily resenting the fact that I was raised with so much physical discipline. I realized that it was something so embedded in my thoughts that I would never be able to have a relationship in which my feelings, and my sexual arousal, and my choices, and my thought patterns weren't tied up in physical consequences. In that period I was outright angry that I couldn't have a simple well-balanced relationship like other females did.

Q: Do you still feel like that?

Marianna: No, not at all. The more I talked to girls who were in simple well-balanced relationships the more I discovered they were as boring as fuck and would never want to be them. When they talked about their boyfriends it put me to sleep. Or I found out they were just pretending everything was picture-perfect but were ten times more screwed up than I was. I began to like the fact that I had grown up in this intense and confusing setting. It suddenly felt more real and human and honest. There was nothing soft and phony about it. My stepfather and my mother were acting on deeper impulses of what they wanted and needed to survive. The only thing that I craved more of from men was love and Andres gives that to me. He whips my butt when I need it but he's not self-serving about it. He does it for my own good and talks about everything to me afterward. I know he'd never discipline me out of sheer anger and he'd never let me get away with anything that I shouldn't be getting away with it.

Q: So tell me about the spanking.

Marianna: Oh my God. I had no idea how bad it was going to be. When my stepfather came over to Andres' house, I was made to wait in the other room while they talked. They discussed my drunk driving incident but also talked about all the reasons I got spanked as a teenager. It was like the two most significant men in my life openly spoke of something that is never openly spoken of. I felt like they were in the same spanking cult or something.

Anyway, after about fifteen minutes, Andres told me to come out. I saw the angry look in my stepfather's eyes and it was like I was living under his roof once again. Andres had the strap in his hand and he ordered me to get a chair from the kitchen. I had butterflies racing in my belly. It was all so intense. I put the chair in the living room and I was told to bare myself. I pulled down my pants and underwear with my back to them. There was such a strange mixture of humiliation and sexual tension. It occurred to me at that instant that I not only sought my stepfather's consequences but I sought him as a man.

He scolded me for the incident and told me I knew better than to make choices like that. He said that he did his best to raise me and he knew in his heart I would never do such a thing again. A few moments of silence passed and then Andres suddenly lashed the strap across my bare butt. He did it quite hard, harder than my stepfather ever had. I was told to get on my toes and get my butt in the air. The feelings that were going through me were so extreme. It was like this collection of emotions of humiliation and pleasure and pain. It was like I was my daddy's naughty girl but it was okay. I was going to take what I had earned and the slate would be wiped clean. The guilt would be gone and I could be a good girl again. Andres would be there to make sure of it.

But then the strapping started getting incredibly heavy. He even started whipping it across the top of my thighs which hurt like hell. I just suddenly burst into tears. All the emotion and pain were too much. It was really cathartic just to cry. I was sobbing as Andres kept spanking me furiously. After he finally stopped, I was sent back out of the room. I kept crying for a while. I heard my stepfather leave.

Q: What happened after that?

Marianna: Well, Andres came in a few minutes later and hugged and kissed me. I clung on to him and promised to never do anything like that again. His words were so soothing after the harsh whipping. I had never experienced anything like that in my life. It all felt so good for everything to be out in the open. I knew then that I didn't ever have to hide anything from him. And I knew that my mother and stepfather would be proud to see me make something of myself and be with a man who they could trust to take care of me.

After that night, we started to date more seriously and six months later he proposed to me. We are now happily married.

Q: Were there more spankings?

Marianna: Yes, I get it semi-regularly when he thinks I need it or deserve it. I ended up in law school so it really helped me get through the tougher days of that, especially when I had to take the BAR exam. I know it's a rather unique thing for a grown women to need to be spanked in order to do her best, but it is the world in which I thrive so I really don't care what anyone else thinks when it comes down to it.

Q: Have you gotten it in front of your stepfather again?

Marianna: Yes, a few times – once when we were over at my parent's place. I had too much to drink and started mouthing off to my husband. He took me into the other room and put me over his knee right there. I think it really pleased my mother. She had a glowing smile on her face at the dinner table after that. I think she sometimes stops by our place just to see if he is going to give me one in front of her. It has all started to become a joke in the family about how much I get it. I like that everything is out in the open. After I met my husband, I stopped feeling like such a weirdo for fantasizing about it all the time. Now, I'm just a good wifey who loves to be kept in line with Daddy's old razor strap that hangs outside my bedroom door once again.

Helena T., *San Diego, CA*

Q: Tell me about your experiences getting spanked.

Helena: I always had spanking fantasies growing up. Maybe it had something to do with being adopted. I don't know. Perhaps there was a need in me from early on to have that feeling of physical connection.

Q: What do you mean?

Helena: I've always longed for this feeling of total trust and lifelong love in a relationship. I think, somehow, that spanking became a fetish for me that incarnates that desire. It takes all the gray areas of desire and makes them very black and white in a physical way.

I've always asked my boyfriends to spank me. Even in high school, I would intentionally piss off my boyfriend and get him to do it. As the years went on, it was just something that I wanted as part of any serious relationship. That's how I met my fiancé.

Q: How did you meet exactly?

Helena: It was a little bit random and a little bit intentional. He was trying to pass by me at a bar and he gave me a light tap on my butt. It was like love at first sight. He did it out of some kind of deep habit but he was also drunk. It didn't matter, though. It got my attention, he bought me a drink and we started talking. I tried to act sassy toward him and he just stared at me like he knew exactly what I was trying to pull. Without even saying a word, he led me to the back of the bar where there were a number of private restrooms. He just took me inside, turned me around, lifted up my skirt and started to spank me. There were a lot of unsaid desires. It was crazy. I'm sure people outside the restroom heard but that made it all the more exhilarating.

Q: How were things after that?

Helena: It's been interesting. We began to see each other right away and he spanked me often from the very beginning. We both have a fetish for vintage everything and that 1950's lifestyle where the man is in charge and the woman plays the role of this submissive goodie-goodie but is super naughty behind closed doors. He has an extensive list of rules for me and has quite a collection of spanking implements.

Q: Like what?

Helena: Lots of vintage and antique things. Ping pong paddles from the 50's, a leather prison strap used in the 19th century on convicts, a vintage cane from an old English boarding school, this old wood paddle that was used to comb cotton, a wicker carpet beater, thick yardsticks from the 20's...things like that. He even has this one implement that was made to be used to herd cattle. That's so embarrassing. I would never tell anyone about that. He likes to use different ones for different reasons. Some of them I like while others I really don't enjoy. He likes to separate pleasure spankings from disciplinary ones so he spanks me accordingly.

Q: What about the rules?

Helena: When we met, I was working at this marketing job that I hated but was afraid to quit. At first, he just encouraged me to quit and do something I really liked. But when he saw that I kept putting off the day I was going to give notice, he took me aside one morning before work. He left the room and came back with this big wooden fraternity paddle. He knew I was terrified of those things. They just look like they could really do some serious damage if you don't know what you are doing. He told me that I would get 20 strokes each day before work and 20 strokes when I got home from work as long as I was working at the job. I threw a fit and said anything and everything to avoid him spanking me with it.

In the end, he had to bend me over his workbench in his garage and tie my hands to the bottom so I wouldn't run away after the first stroke. After 20 strokes, not only was my butt thoroughly beaten but my face was covered in perspiration from trying to take the pain. I could hardly sit down that day. And then he gave me another 20 when I got home. I nearly threw up. After three days of this, I broke down in tears to him and told him that I was terrified to quit. It was more of an emotional fear of the unknown but the spanking just forced it out. He promised to support my decision and help me out to get started on my new career.

Q: And what was that?

Helena: A catering business specializing in nouveau American cuisine. The logo was this slutty-looking June Cleaver image and all the girls I hired wore these cute swing dresses with a red print. I think we got lots of kinky housewives as customers just from the marketing.

Q: How did he help you get started?

Helena: We decided to move in together which was the biggest step. That came with me totally submitting to his rules. It was a full-on kinky take on the 1950's lifestyle like you've never seen.

Q: How so?

Helena: I was to have dinner on the table at seven, or I was spanked with his belt. I was to always be dressed to please—pencil skirts, vintage playsuits, little cocktail dresses, waist-cinching corsets and sometimes just a little white apron with nothing on underneath. If he didn't like it, he hand-spanked me over the back of the sofa and then kept me naked for the rest of the evening. After I came up with a business plan for the catering company, he kept me on a strict schedule for getting it off the ground. He was really harsh with me on getting the first clients. He would spank me with one of his canes if he thought I wasn't trying hard enough. He works as an industrial designer so knows how to make all kinds of wild devices.

Q: Like what?

Helena: He built this stainless steel spreader that he puts me in if he thinks I've been especially naughty. It holds me on my hands and knees with these thick metal locks that go around my wrists and ankles. I can't move at all and it drives me crazy. He spanks me when I'm in it and it makes me so horny because I am so restrained. He gets me really turned on with spankings and touching me, and then just leaves me there to suffer if I've been bad. One time, he left me in it all night. That was torture.

Q: What does the spanking do for you?

Helena: It mostly makes me really horny. The bad ones really hurt and I don't like them at all. It's this strange paradox that the same thing brings me both intense pleasure and intense pain. I like how it is always there, though. It's like a sign of caring that I can't explain. If he stopped wanting to spank me, our relationship would be over.

Q: How have you been spanked recently?

Helena: My fiancé sent me to etiquette school. He knew this woman who is really into spanking and discipline as well. I have classes twice a week. She teaches me how to walk properly, speak like a proper aristocratic servant, set the dinner table for French royalty…things like that. He gave her permission to discipline me and she whips me with a crop when I make a mistake. It's really kinky.

Venus L., *Quebec, Canada*

Q: Tell me about your experiences getting spanked.

Venus: I've always had this thing for white guys. I grew up in a suburb of Quebec that was mostly middle-upper class and upper class. Our family wasn't poor but we definitely weren't rich either as my parents were immigrants from Haiti. I think it made me conflicted. I was a very prissy black girl who wanted a luxurious lifestyle and always ended up dating white boys who tended to have more money. But as I got into my twenties, I was really dissatisfied with my vanilla relationships. The guys always treated me like a princess because that's how I acted, but I also developed these constant urges to be objectified. I would fantasize constantly about being a man's possession and always longed to be spanked during sex or just to be spanked because I wanted him to take me physically.

Q: Did you ever tell the guys that?

Venus: No, never. It wasn't that I was just embarrassed about expressing the feelings but I wanted a man who just treated me like that naturally. I didn't really know how to reconcile the feelings until I started exploring the world of BDSM and found this whole sub-culture of men who liked to own women like slaves. It seemed so taboo that it was as if it was illegal. Some of the couples involved totally shocked me. I remember seeing a photo of this white guy with his black girlfriend in a cage next to him. It took me days just to get over the shock. But it also gave me this sensation that was so undeniable.

Q: What did you do?

Venus: I started to chat with men online and went to a few local gatherings but I never really connected with anyone. Then one night, I was randomly chatting with people and started to talk with this guy who said he was a stockbroker who lived in Connecticut, just outside New York. He sent me some photos and he was really attractive. He had deep blue eyes and this clean-cut All-American look. He told me what he wanted and it was like he was describing my deepest fantasies.

Q: What did he say?

Venus: He said he wanted a woman who was smart and independent but at the same time was his to own and control. His exact words were he wanted "a piece of black meat who knows she needs to be spanked like a slave." I've never had a guy talk to me like that. He was very intelligent which was a turn-on but it was more how he described how I would be treated. He expected to me have a career but he would own me in all ways like his slave. He would decide how I dressed, control the look of my body, train my mind to think how he wanted it to think, discipline me as he saw fit and so on. I would be his de facto slave.

To say that to a black woman brings up some intense thoughts but he wasn't looking to make me his slave because he thought I was inferior. He desired emotionally, psychologically and physically to own a woman completely. It was so extreme but it spoke to me. It was spanking taken to another level of physical control. Plus, on the lighter side, we could talk about things such as music and politics. Most men like this are so far out in the twilight zone of

BDSM that they can't function in a relationship that exists in the larger world of life and human connection.

Q: So how did it proceed?

Venus: We talked on the phone for some time but both of us realized we needed to meet in order to see if there was something real between us. It was early December and he asked me if I had ever been to Mont Tremblant, a ski resort close to Montreal. It was a short flight from New York for him and he said he was in dire need of a good winter vacation. I was hesitant, at first, meeting a total stranger there but the impulsive romanticism of meeting a man who might want to own me made me say yes.

We decided on dates and he made the reservation. It didn't take him long to send me a list of what I was to bring to wear—tight white ski pants, a g-string for the hotel spa and skimpy plunge dresses for dinner at night. I was oozing with kinky excitement but I didn't really know what to expect. Even a few days before the departure date, I was having second thoughts and almost canceled. You get caught up in online fantasies and then the reality of making the effort for a total stranger catches up with you. In the end, I got in my car and drove to meet him at the resort hotel.

Q: So how did it go?

Venus: I got there before he did and checked into our room. When he landed at the airport, he called me and asked me how everything was. I read him a ski report on the snow conditions and told him about the amenities at the resort. He told me to make a reservation at the hotel restaurant and then strip down bare to wait for him to arrive and inspect me. I asked him in shock, "Inspect me?" He told me he wanted to inspect my body to see if it pleased him. It was so blunt and carnal. I suddenly felt like it was not a romantic rendezvous but a pleasure vacation for him to inspect "a piece of black meat" to see if he wanted to own it. My emotions were mixed. It made me want to turn off my mind and go with it. I was not only meeting a total stranger but I was to wait in the hotel room for him completely naked.

Q: Did you do it?

Venus: Yes. It was so exhilarating to pace around the room totally nude while I waited for him to arrive. I was so nervous and wondered what would happen if he didn't like my body. Would he just send me on my way? I had never done something like this. He sent me a text message that he had just walked into the hotel lobby and that he was on his way up. I waited anxiously at the door for him until I heard him knock. I opened the door and peeked around it to conceal my body. He looked so sexy. He was wearing a gray wool winter jacket and thick black corduroy pants. Very stylish. He had a short crew cut that gave him an almost military look. We greeted each other, and he entered and closed the door.

I tried to cover my breasts with one arm and had my other hand between my legs. He told me he would inspect me formally right now and we could get to know each other for dinner. He looked me up and down and then placed his hand on my shoulder to turn me around. He suddenly spanked me across my bare ass and told me to put my arms down. I immediately dropped them. He turned me back around and told me not to cover myself again, that I should get used to being a naked black slave. His words turned me on so badly.

He began to inspect each part of my body. He fondled each of my breasts and nipples, ran his hands across the curves of my hips, grabbed to see if I had any fat on my body, and then made me open up my mouth to inspect my teeth. I felt so self-conscious. He had all the power. He told me to turn around and squat down. I did and I could feel him ogling my ass from behind. He told me to flex each cheek, first one side and then the other. I felt like a porno girl. He kept making me do it over and over, and then he asked me to shake my ass up and down. It became humiliating and I laughed.

When he heard me laugh, he suddenly went to his bag and searched through it to find something. I turned and saw him pull out a leather strap. He marched toward me, arched it back and slapped it hard across my bare ass. I gasped in pain but he did it several more times. He asked me if I thought something was funny. I was truly scared for a moment. I mean I didn't know what he was capable of and here he was spanking me really harshly with this thick leather strap. I told him no and wiped the smile from my face. He told me to shake my ass up and down until he told me I could stop. I did but when I got a bit tired, he spanked me again. He finally told me to stand up again.

He inspected my face and body for a couple more minutes. He asked me if I had any objections to modifying my body. I didn't know what he meant exactly but I was afraid to ask. I told him no. Eventually, he stopped, smiled at me and told me that I was a nice piece of meat. I smiled back and thanked him. He went back to his bag and searched through it again. He took out this really nice silver choker necklace. He wrapped it around my neck and clasped it in place. He told me that I was his for the weekend and we could see how things went after that. I walked over to the mirror and looked at myself. I really did look like a slave standing there naked with the choker around my neck. I couldn't believe I was going through with this. None of my friends had any idea I craved such a thing and would die if they saw me like that.

Q: So how did the weekend go?

Venus: It was incredible. We completely connected even on a normal level. We skied, went out for dinner, and spent the nights in our hotel room. He began to train me the way he wanted me to be. It was really difficult for me to get used to at first. I am normally very assertive and just do what I want. The first evening, I told him I was going to take a bath. He stopped me, told me I needed to ask him to do anything and for me to bend over right there to get whipped. He took his strap and thrashed my bare butt until I was nearly in tears.

There were lots of instances like that. When we went out for dinner, he had me wear this plunge dress that was made to be worn without a bra. We stayed indoors and ate at the hotel restaurant, but anyone could see my cold, hard nipples poking through. I clung to his arm wherever we went. At night, we had some really kinky sex. He would talk really dirty to me, telling me things like, "I need to have my mouth trained to suck white cock," while he made me gag and spanked me for not being able to deep-throat him. He totally treated me like his slut and I loved it. He was the first man who treated me so possessively and roughly, but still liked the finer things in life. It felt like he resolved the conflicts inside of me.

Q: How about after that?

Venus: The weekend ended perfectly. He told me that he would fly me to Connecticut the next weekend and we began to talk nightly. A month later, he told me to start looking for a job near him. It all happened so fast but we were really into each other. I just did whatever he told me to do. A couple of months later I moved in with him and really started to live like his slave.

Q: What did that consist of?

Venus: He began to control everything and I received strict discipline for any rule-breaking or failure to meet his demands. He spanked me with various paddles, straps, canes, and even a horsewhip. I would be spanked daily at times. I could wear what I needed to for work, but apart from that, he decided. He began to modify my body as well. He bought me custom waist-cinching corsets and started me on a schedule to make my waist smaller. He wanted hardcore curves on me. He limited my diet, set my gym schedule and inspected me weekly.

He made me wear the corset to work and would make it tighter and tighter. I nearly fainted at work one time. Over the course of several months, my physical figure slowly changed. I felt like one of those women you see in photos from foreign countries with the ornamental metal neck braces. He also put me in various restraints that he had purchased. He has antique slave shackles, wood stocks, real metal slave collars from the 19th century, vintage dog collars, and all sorts of other things. Sometimes he has me wear this kinky contraption. It's a thick metal collar connected by an industrial-grade chain to a metal anal hook. Then he adds this little white apron and high heels. He makes me cook dinner like that sometimes. It looks so outrageous. It's like extreme dress-up.

When I first moved in, before I started my new job, he put me through this period of being brainwashed. I was locked in a spreader most of the night and sleep-deprived. I would be spanked every hour of the day that he was home. He would whip me and ask me over and over to convince him that I really believed that I was his piece of black slave meat. I nearly went crazy.

Q: Did you like it?

Venus: Well, there are parts that I didn't like, but yes. I felt like I was owned like his possession. Plus, most of my friends had just boring suburban lives. He always makes the daily rituals of life into something sexually exhilarating. When I'm at work, trudging through some marketing report, all I can think about is what he has in store for me when I get home. I love it. Even when we are out with friends, it only takes a sly smack on my ass to get me going.

Carly J., *San Pedro, CA*

Q: Tell me about your experiences getting spanked.

Carly: I'd gotten it growing up and I later got spanked by a couple of boyfriends, but there was one experience that I'll never forget.

Q: What happened?

Carly: I grew up in a very working-class neighborhood. It seemed like everyone worked at the shipping port or was a cop or mechanic, or something like that. There was a general old-school mentality to how parents raised kids. Well, my best friend at the time was the type of girl who always got me into trouble but I kept hanging out with her because she was so much fun. Also, her dad was a firefighter and I totally had a crush on him. He seemed like a hero out of the movies riding around in the front seat of the fire engine. He looked so strong and invincible. He had thick black hair and olive-colored skin. He and my dad were also friends so he would come over to our house occasionally for BBQs.

Q: So something happened with him?

Carly: Yes. I was 18 at the time and in my senior year in high school. After school one day, my friend got a hold of some pot and we went to her house to smoke it in her backyard. She lived at the edge of this preserve so there weren't that many neighbors who could see or smell it. Her dad was on one of his 12-hour shifts and wouldn't be home until late that night. Or so we thought.

I guess someone smelled the smoke or something and called the fire department. It was like the worst combination of coincidences you can imagine. We heard the sirens but it wasn't until they were outside the house that we realized they were there. We had already finished the joint and were just sitting there acting high. All of a sudden, these firefighters, including her dad, came out of the back door of her house and we were speechless. We quickly realized what happened. Her dad asked her if there was a fire and then he suddenly smelled the lingering pot smoke. His eyes nearly popped out of his face he was so angry. He yelled at both of us to get in the house. The other firefighters were laughing as they exited out the front door but her dad was so embarrassed and angry that they would get called to his own house.

As we moved past him to go inside, he shouted at my friend, "I am going to spank your butt raw for this." I had never heard someone say that. Then he looked at me and told me to call my dad right now and hand him the phone. I was obviously scared to tell my dad but I was afraid of the two of them talking about what happened.

Q: So what happened then?

Carly: I called my dad on my cell phone, told him I got in trouble, and handed my friend's dad the phone. I was scared of what he was going to say but the whole situation seemed like a dream. I was still high from the pot so watching my friend's dad stand there in his full firefighter's outfit was almost funny to me. He noticed the smile and he shouted at me in anger, "Wipe that smile off your face!" My heart jumped when he said it. So, he told my dad over the phone what happened and that he's about the give his daughter the spanking of her life. When he said this, my dad said something back to him on the phone that I couldn't hear, but it made him look up at me while he listened. I started to panic the more they talked and seemed to be agreeing to something.

He handed me back the phone and my dad told me I was going to get whatever punishment my friend's dad was going to give her. At first, I thought he meant my dad was going to spank me but when I looked up at my friend's dad, I realized that he meant him. I was so confused. It had been years since I got one, but it was more the fact of another man spanking me that seemed to cross a line I had never thought could be crossed. I was also in disbelief that my dad would allow it. It felt like some guy thing I would expect from other men but to have my own dad give permission to spank me was scary in some deep way.

Q: So what did he do?

Carly: After I hung up the phone, her dad pointed at both of us with opposite hands and shouted, "Over the back of the couch, now! I'm going to get my belt!" I looked up at my friend in astonishment. I think she felt worse for me and embarrassed that her dad would do this. I could still hear the loud hum of the fire engine from outside. The rest of the crew were waiting for him. My friend and I just stood at the back of the couch in a state of paralysis. I remember asking her if he was really going to do it and she said yes. Then I asked her if he spanks hard and she just nodded with this look of pain on her face.

A few seconds later, her dad came storming back down the stairs, trouncing across the living room in his firefighter pants. He had taken off his jacket and just wore a white T-shirt underneath. He had a thick brown leather belt in his hand. He glared at me and said, "You first. Get your jeans down now and bend over that couch before I get my paddle." When he said that, I became terrified. I looked over at my friend but she didn't know what to say. Her dad told her to wait for her turn against the wall. I felt almost sick to my stomach, but I moved to undo my jeans and pull them down. I remember I was wearing a little thong so my whole butt was totally exposed to her dad. It was so humiliating at the time.

I bent over the coach and dug my hands into the back of the cushions. I glanced behind me and saw him straightening the belt in his hands in preparation. He caught me looking at him and ordered me to look forward. He wasted no time in laying the belt into me. He spanked me hard from the very first stroke and my body jerked forward. He started scolding me for doing drugs at his house. My head was pushed down into the cushions and I couldn't see when the spankings were going to come. I would just tense up, the stinging sensation would suddenly whip across my bare butt and I would exhale in and out to recover. That happened over and over about 50 times. Then he told me to stand up and pull up my pants. It was over. He sent me into the other room as he spanked his daughter.

Q: What happened after that?

Carly: He just finished with my friend and then he left. On the way out, he told me I needed to go home. I watched him as he stormed back outside, climbed into the fire rig, and drove off.

Q: What did your dad say?

Carly: Nothing really. He knew it would shock me and it did. He just said that I better not think about smoking weed again. I told him I wouldn't and I went to my room. I was really angry at him at the time but more confused about getting it from my friend's dad.

Q: What did you think about it in retrospect?

Carly: For the first few days, I just kept playing it back in my mind over and over. When I imagined it again, there was no pain. There was just the exhilaration of having her dad tell me to pull down my jeans and the feeling of the powerful strokes of his belt across my bare ass. It turned me on in a weird way. In fact, I was afraid to go over there again and be confronted by him. I felt like we both did something wrong. My friendship with his daughter even began to fall apart after that. We just stopped doing things together.

Later on, though, I mean months and years after, the image was still stuck in my head. It is purely sexual now. I love to fantasize about it and I even seek out older guys who are into spanking. It's like I want that type of guy- the kind of man who just spanks his woman without a second thought. I even have become more and more turned on by exhibitionism lately. I don't know if it's solely because of that or if I had that desire in me already, but the feeling of being exposed and exhibited for others to see really turns me on. I wear more revealing clothes now and even gave a boyfriend a blow job in front of his friends one time. I don't want to say it was all because of this spanking. I think I was wired to like spanking before it even happened. That just brought it out in full force.

Ashley O., *New York, NY*

Q: Tell me about your experiences getting spanked.

Ashley: I've always liked a little slap on the ass during wild sex but there was this one intense fling I had with a guy that really made me feel what a spanking was all about.

Q: Tell me about it.

Ashley: I was at this swank party in Soho with a couple of my friends. It was in the loft of a well-known actress whose director-boyfriend had just premiered his first film at the Angelica. There was that vibe that made you feel like you were surrounded by the most attractive men in the city. It was just a mixture of all sorts of people—Wall Street types, ad men, magazine editors, models, film producers, hip-hop artists…It was as if someone had handpicked the crowd. I was single, drunk and just enjoying the night.

Q: So what happened?

Ashley: So I'm waiting in a crowd of people at the bar that was set up there, trying to get a drink, and I suddenly feel someone's hand run across the small of my back. I turn and this guy suddenly slips by me to the front of the bar. He says, "Thanks," in this snobby English accent, and goes to order a drink. I couldn't believe it. He turns back to me and starts laughing. He gives me this mock apology and then asks me what I'd like to drink. He's smirking the whole time. I wanted to slap him. He was smug and full of himself, but he was also attractive as hell. He had green eyes, a layer of scruff on his face, and really prominent facial features like an old-school boxer. He was wearing a black jacket and jeans. He acted like he didn't give a shit about pretensions in that rebellious English sort of way. He told me he was a venture capitalist and rambled off the names of all these companies I had never heard of.

We started talking really intensely about art and money and how people act when they are around it. The whole time he was talking to me, he kept touching me. At first, it was just casual brushes on my hip or my hand, but then he began to draw really close to me, and touched me on my back and ran his hand along the top of my thigh. It made me feel a bit comfortable but at the same time, I liked his physical attraction to me. It was as if he needed to touch me to get his point across.

Q: So what happened then?

Ashley: So in the middle of the conversation, which had gotten really intense at this point, he whispers in my ear, "Let's go." I just looked at him and replied, "Are you serious? I just met you an hour ago." He glared back at me, wrapped his hand around the small of my back, and said again, "Let's go." It was like an invitation but also felt like an order. He was aggressive but confident in a carefree way. My reaction went through these layers of mind in a split second. It was like I went from "I just met you" to "I don't know anything about you" to "I've never met anyone like you" to "Should I be scared of you?" to "I just want you to make me go with you." He grabbed my hand and took me. I sent a text to my friend that I was leaving with a random Englishman I just met.

We got inside the elevator. There was another couple in there but this guy didn't care. He started kissing me and fondling me right in front of them. Then, he slaps me on the ass. I mean really hard. He was like some kind of primordial man who just gave in to his physical impulses but spoke like an Eton-educated Englishman. The other couple just glanced at us like we were crazy.

Q: You liked the spanking?

Ashley: Yes, but it was more shocking than anything. When we got out of the elevator, I asked him where he lived. He told me he lived in Midtown but he couldn't wait to get there to fuck me. He said it just like that. We were walking down a dark street heading toward Canal Street when we passed this thin alley. He tugged my hand and before I knew it we were in the alley, he had my back pressed against a brick wall, and he was kissing me deeply. Then, he slapped my ass again. He was so physical I felt like a cavewoman. He spanked it again, and then lifted up my dress, and spanked me bare. I looked up the alley to see if there was anyone there and when I did, he led me further down the alley. We stopped at the edge of this loading dock and suddenly turned me around. He lifted my dress and began to spank me really hard. I don't know how where his ferocity came from but he just wanted to slap my bare ass over and over. It was inexplicable. He just wanted to lay his claim to my body by striking it. It hurt but it was so sexually stimulating.

Q: Were you worried about your safety?

Ashley: I was completely into the moment. He was a predator who had captured his prey and I had already signaled to him by going down the alley that I was his for the taking. He turned me back around and kissed me. I felt his hands go up my dress and pull down my panties. I looked again up the alley to see if there was anyone there. By the time I looked back, he had his pants undone and was pulling out a condom from his wallet. He slipped it on with one hand while he kissed me again. Then he grabbed me with both hands and lifted me up. My legs wrapped around him and he held me up with one arm. I started to ride him up and down as he began to spank me again. It was so savage. He spanked me in between almost every thrust into me. Over and over. I held onto the back of his neck as he fucked me and spanked me. There was nothing delicate about it. He just wanted to have me and make sure I felt it in every way. I was writhing up and down on his body and the more he spanked me, the faster I would ride his cock. It was just a good hard slutty spanking and fucking. There's no other way to describe it.

Elizabeth S., *Charleston, SC*

Q: Tell me about your experiences getting spanked.

Elizabeth: I'd like to say my boyfriend got me into it, but I probably liked it before he did it. He just brought it out. We were dating in college and I was always hanging out at his place. He lived in this big house with three of his good friends. I've always craved attention and liked to wear those little short shorts when I was at his place. Well, one day, when I was wearing them, we were all sitting around watching a football game. I stood up to get something to drink and out of nowhere, he smacked my ass with his hand. He told me to go get him a beer. He was kind of joking but it was in front of his roommates and they all took notice. I told him not to do it but it wasn't in a very convincing manner. He told his roommates that it's okay, that I like to be spanked. I yelled at him and walked out of the room.

Q: So what happened?

Elizabeth: So, the next semester, my boyfriend left to study abroad. We hadn't really been seeing each other that long and it wasn't super serious, but we expected to stay together while he was gone. Well, we started to get into arguments on all these emotional long-distance calls and he ended up breaking up with me. I was so upset and surprised. I thought he had met someone else while he was abroad. So, a couple of weeks later, I went to his place to pick up my things. When I got there, all his roommates were in the living room watching a game and drinking. When I came down the stairs, one of them asked me to come over to him. I asked him why and he just told me to come to him. When I got there, he grabbed me and

131

spanked me. He told me to go get him a beer. I laughed sarcastically but then one of his other friends grabbed me and did the same thing. Then, the third added his own spanking. It was funny and I don't think they expected me to go get them but I wanted to see their reaction so I went to get the beers for them. I shouldn't have done it but I did.

Q: Why shouldn't you have done it?

Elizabeth: Because they were just testing me and they were drunk. Once I brought them back the beers, one of them grabbed me and put me over his knee. He started spanking me over my shorts. At first, I laughed and told him to stop, but he didn't stop and I didn't really struggle that much. I should have just left but I didn't. I pretended like he was holding me down against my will and spanking me. He handed me his beer and I took a long swig of it. After that, they knew I was into it. He started spanking me harder. They were really drunk. I was trying to pretend the whole time that I was resisting but guys will just keep at it unless you tell them to stop.

Q: Did you want them to stop?

Elizabeth: No, not at all, but I was feeling immense guilt. These were my boyfriend's friends. It was like I was cheating on him in some way even though we were broken up. But at the same time, I think I had a desire to get back at him in the most vicious way. The fact that I loved to be spanked and had three guys who were manhandling me was just a very convenient excuse.

Q: So they were all spanking you?

Elizabeth: Yeah, they were pushing me back and forth, giving me beer the whole time. I was totally acting like a slut, but at a certain point, I didn't care. One of them pulled my shorts down and started to spank my bare bottom. I could feel him getting hard underneath me. I mean, after he pulled my shorts down, it had to keep going. One of his other friends stood up and came over next to me. They both started spanking me, taking turns to see how red they could make it. Then one of them took my hand and put it on the bulge in his pants. I pulled it back and told him to stop. He grabbed it and did it again, squeezing it around the girth of his dick beneath the khaki pants he was wearing. When he let go of my hand, I kept squeezing it. I was really just a reckless slut at this point.

He let me grope him for a couple of minutes and then suddenly unzipped his pants. He slipped his hard cock out the slit in his boxers. I was like, "Oh my God, no, I can't." He was so aroused, though, that he just grabbed my hand and put it on his dick. His friend spanked me hard again and it just sent me over the edge. I started stroking it and then titled my head up to put it in my mouth. The guys were all going crazy and this point. They looked at each other, encouraging me to do it and talking to me dirty. The guy whose lap I was on suddenly pulled my panties down and slipped his fingers in me. I was already so wet from the spanking.

The guy I was going down on grabbed the back of my head and pulled it toward him. His cock went so far down my throat that I gagged. His friend says, "Spank her and make her deep-throat." I protested and told them that I couldn't deep-throat but they didn't care. They moved me to the end of the couch so I was on my knees and leaning over the edge. One of them grabbed my hands and held them behind my back. They were totally manhandling me. I started to suck one of them and he tried to make me deep throat him. When I gagged again, the other spanked me several times. It was overwhelming. One guy held my head, the other held my arms behind my back and the third spanked me. They were so aroused that I was actually doing this that it just made them hornier.

The spanker reached into my legs and started to fondle my clit. I immediately started writhing in pleasure but they held me down. He rubbed me really fast while he spanked me. I thought I was going to have an orgasm in a matter of seconds. I couldn't believe I was doing this. I had never done anything like that and have never done anything since. It was just the moment and the fact that I knew them. I had drunk enough to lose any inhibitions as well. I think I really just needed to feel desired after my boyfriend broke up with me. The spankings were just proof that they wanted me. Having all three of them take turns spanking me was like an orgy of desire. It made me want to just totally submit to being slutty.

Q: So how did it end?

Elizabeth: Like you would expect. They all came. I had two orgasms. They were so turned on that it didn't take them long to come. They held me down and made me swallow. So dirty. I still can't believe to this day that I did it. After it was over, I went to the bathroom and washed my mouth out twenty times. My ass was bright red and hurt for days after that. I made them swear not to tell anyone about it. I never went over there again and avoided them at school. The image stays with me, though. After that, I would really get off on being spanked when I was giving head to my other boyfriends. It was my one night of sluthood that will always stick with me.

Kate G., New York, NY

Q: Tell me about your experiences getting spanked.

Kate: I grew up in upstate New York and moved to the city to go to school. It was the first time that I had lived away from home. A friend of a friend was looking for another roommate in her three-bedroom apartment and it was really cheap so I told her I would take it without even looking at it. When I got there, I found out she had a male roommate. It was actually his apartment and he was the only one on the lease. I already had issues with being on my own. My father was very overly protective and kind of controlling. I rebelled against it but when it came down to it, I was used to him telling me what I could and couldn't do. Once I moved in with another guy, I think I was looking for someone to keep me grounded. Plus, he was good looking and there was a sexual tension between us the first time we met.

Q: So what happened?

Kate: I felt this need...this need for him to look out for me. I was really unsure of myself and I had always had this strong male presence in my life. I didn't know how to interact with guys except to rebel against them or seek their acceptance. So, one day when he was leaving and asked him if I could talk with him. He casually agreed. I didn't know what to say to express what I needed. The way it came out was that I asked him if he could teach me.

Q: Teach you?

Kate: Yes. I was studying to be a teacher and it was my mentality. He asked me what I meant and I said that if he

135

felt like he needed to teach me something that I was fine with that. He just gave me a weird look, said okay, and left. It didn't come across how I wanted it to come across at all.

Q: How did you want it to come across?

Kate: I don't know. I wanted him to be my mentor in some way, but he already had his own life. He was a few years older, was heavily involved in his job in the publishing industry and he had a girlfriend. So, instead of letting it go, I started to act out. I would play my music really loud, leave my dishes unwashed, take his mail…things like that. He got increasingly irritated until finally he told me we needed to have a talk. He was really upset at the time. I told him again that I just wanted him to teach me. He told me that the only thing he felt like teaching me at that moment was to whip my ass. I looked him in the eye and told him that "whatever he felt I needed was fine with me." It was a very intense moment. He was just speaking freely when he said it, but I had triggered the reaction I was looking for in some way. A few seconds passed without either of us saying anything and then he just said, "Get up."

I asked him why and he repeated the words, "Get up." He grabbed me by the arm and took me to my room. He told me that he was going to really teach me. I got all emotional, asking him what he thought he was doing, but deep down, it was exactly what I wanted. But I couldn't really tell him that, so I struggled and protested. He took me to my room and slammed the door. Our other roommate wasn't home so it was dramatic when he closed the door. Before he even said anything, he unclasped his belt and whipped it out of his pants. I still remember the sound of it whisking against the fabric of his jeans as he tore it from the belt loops. It made a strong impression on me and I just looked up at him in fear.

Q: What did you think he was going to do?

Kate: I don't know. For a moment, I thought he was just going to swing it at me. I could feel my hands shaking. Then he said, "Turn around." I asked him why. I was always the type to protest to the end. He told me to turn around again and I told him no. He grabbed me and tried to turn me around, but I took hold of his arms and struggled like crazy. It was really intense and physical. He finally picked me up and threw me on my bed. He held me down and then climbed on my back so I couldn't move. I was wearing black leggings and he grabbed a hold of them at the waist. I held onto them with my hands so he took my arms and pinned them under his knees. This all happened in a matter of seconds. It was like a fight. I kept asking him what he was doing and telling him that I wasn't scared of him.

Q: Did you want to be scared of him?

Kate: Probably. Yes. I tend to only do things after I fight against doing them and someone makes me do them. I don't know why. I just need to feel like they care enough to really subdue me and make me do it. It's very immature, I know, but that's just the way I am wired.

Q: So what happened next?

Kate: He had me completely pinned down so I couldn't move, but he had dropped his belt on the floor during the struggle so he just started to spank me with his hand. I kept calling out his name, asking him what he thought he was doing, but he just spanked me and told me that he was going to teach me. He was just really fed up with all of my acting out. After a couple of minutes, the spanking really started to hurt. He was striking his palm against my bare butt with all his strength. He really wanted me to feel it. So it got to a point where I said, "Fine, I'll do what you tell me." It was what I was looking to happen. I just needed to feel that he really was going to keep doing it until I submitted to him. In a weird way, I felt like I was controlling the situation because I wanted his commitment to me. I wanted him to pay attention to me and to be someone who looked after me if I didn't know how to deal with life. He had ignored me so I had acted like a child to aggravate him. I know how silly it is but it is what I need.

Q: What happened after you gave in?

Kate: He climbed off of me and told me to get up. I went to stand up and pull my pants up. He said, "No. Turn around now. I'm not going to tolerate you rebelling like a little girl." I was standing there with my pants around my thighs and I just couldn't give in still. He grabbed me and turned me around. This time, I just kind of gave a half-hearted struggle but he knew that I was taking his direction. He told me to bend over and he pushed me down. He grabbed a hold of my wrists and told me to lock my hands behind my ankles. I bucked up again and he shoved me back down, smacking me hard several times on my ass. I just needed his hands on me or I couldn't do it. Finally, he forced me to assume the position, bent over with my hands interwoven around the backs of my ankles. I watched him pick up his belt, fold it in half and then swing it toward me. It whipped around the full width of my butt and stung like hell. I flinched and started to unclasp my hands. He immediately said, "Don't." He was cued into my reactions.

He whipped me again and I held my hands clasped. He did it probably ten more times and then told me to pull up my pants. I had started to cry and I didn't even realize it. The tears were streaming down my face. He looked at me coldly, almost happy that he had made me cry. The whole event was so powerful. He just walked out of the room and slammed the door behind him.

Q: What was it like after that?

Kate: He came into my room later that night to talk to me. He told me that I needed to start acting more considerate and tell him if I needed him to teach me something. It felt like such an emotional conversation. I just nodded a lot and told him that I was sorry for acting how I did. I felt bad that I had purposely brought it to that point. I promised that I would try to be more direct and thoughtful.

Q: Did you?

Kate: For a while, yes, I did. But I found out that I needed more attention than he was willing to give. He would come home and be occupied doing his own things. Eventually, I got out of control one night and came home at two in the morning and started blasting my music in my room. Our other roommate was out of town and subconsciously I was probably looking for more conflict.

Q: Conflict? You wanted the conflict?

Kate: Yes, I see now that I needed it. If someone doesn't get hands-on with me, I feel really insecure and out of control. I know it sounds psychotic but I do it over and over. I'm fine with it. I just need someone who understands that.

Q: Did he understand that?

Kate: Yes and no. He came in that night in a rage and spanked me to tears again. It was almost the same scenario. I think he knew then that it was just a ritual that I needed. Act out, get spanked and cry. The next day, he knocked on my door and he gave me a list of rules printed out on a piece of paper. He told me to put it tape it to my wall. It listed all these rules about my behavior and what I was allowed to do and not to do. I really liked that he took the time to do it. But in the end, I realized he was just trying to solve the situation and I was looking for more and more conflict. He had a girlfriend and even if he wanted to get involved with me, he couldn't.

Q: You wanted to be with him?

Kate: Yes, I think so. I wanted him to totally be into me and be the guy I looked to for everything. He seemed really wise to me even though I'm sure he had his own problems and hang-ups. Even after he put the list up, I would do something, it would get really physical and he would spank me again. It was what I needed- just to be spanked to submission and loved. But after a few months of doing it, he told me that I needed to move out. His girlfriend would come over and she sensed something strange going on. I threw a fit and he spanked me one last time. After that, I didn't even see him until the day I moved out. Even though I've matured a lot since then, I can't help but think that we had a really unique connection and it would have developed if he wasn't seeing someone. I don't know. There is just this fierce desire in me for a man to get physical with me. I need it badly.

Valentina P., *Bradenton, FL*

Q: Tell me about your experiences getting spanked.

Valentina: I grew up in a traditional Russian household, but I really didn't get any memorable spankings, at least ones I can remember. But I also grew up on the tennis court so in some ways I was closer to my coach than to my own father. He was Russian, too, though but he had been in America for more than 20 years so he had learned to temper his harsh attitude. In Russia, people just understand that you have to go through extreme training in order to be the best. If you have to be punished, so what? The ends justified the means. In America, people are a lot more concerned about living a balanced life, but a balanced life doesn't win the championship at Wimbledon. Nikolai was a lot more flexible with his American and European students, but he knew I was Russian so he felt like he could resort to traditional values.

Q: What were traditional values for him?

Valentina: Do what you are told, and do it well, or you'll suffer the consequences. I had a sponsor who was paying my expenses in the junior ranks and he expected me to move into the top 100 in the world when I entered the professional circuit. There were times when I was a junior when things got physical, but I don't want to talk about it. Plus, it was minor compared to what he did after I was a professional player.

Q: What did he do?

Valentina: Nikolai believed that in order for a person to reach their true physical potential, they had to be pushed through "thresholds" as he called them. He said that people would make the same mistakes over and over but keep expecting different results unless they were properly corrected. For him, proper correction meant physical discipline that mentally altered an individual. Russians pride themselves on being able to endure anything. So, for the discipline to truly work, it had to be extreme. In Stalin's time, men were sent to Siberia and only the strong ones survived starvation. For female Russian tennis players, from early Communist times up to today, there was a similar mentality, only not so crazy. Elite athletes are honored not only for their skill but for their glorification of Mother Russia.

Q: You still didn't tell me what he did.

Valentina: There were certain training days, that, if I didn't perform to expectation, I would be taken somewhere private and caned.

Q: Caned?

Valentina: Yes. It is the way some Russians like to punish. It is like the big wooden paddle in America, but the intent is to inflict a very harsh and visible result. I've seen young women who get thirty or forty strokes that are so forcefully administered that you can see the blood welling up on the welts. It is no joke.

Q: This happened to you?

Valentina: Yes. Nikolai didn't believe in doing anything half-way. I was ranked in the top ten in the junior ranks, but when I turned professional I had a hard time just getting out of the first couple of rounds in minor tournaments. My serve wasn't strong enough and my ground game wasn't quick enough. We had several arguments on the court and then finally there was this one day that reached the boiling point. It was late in the evening and all his other students had left. I had been pushing myself harder and harder but it just wasn't enough. After I sent one forehand ten meters over the fence, Nikolai told me that he had enough and sent me to the locker room.

I was so upset. I went inside, sat down on one of the benches and started crying. When I heard him come in, I was totally shocked. He never came into the female locker room, but no one else was there. He already had the cane in his hand and started yelling at me to stop crying like a little girl. He grabbed me by the arm and told me to stand up. I was still crying but he ordered me to bend over. He took my racket and placed it behind my ankles. He told me, in Russian, to hold onto it until he was finished. I grasped it so my arms were locked behind my legs. He flipped up my skirt and pulled down my tennis under-shorts in this really rough way. I stopped crying because I felt like it was going to be worse if I acted like a baby.

Q: How did you act?

Valentina: I just took it. I knew that I deserved it. I mean nothing else was working. He had already told me to believe in myself and my potential many times, but it only took me so far. He knew that the sheer fear of real pain was the last chance at pushing me to another level. I just bared it.

Q: What did he do exactly?

Valentina: He gave me a quick scolding. He told me very formally that I deserved to be punished for my behavior on the court. He said that if I can't take a little pain then I shouldn't come back the next day. He whipped it across my bare butt for the first time. It was so much more excruciating than I had imagined it would be. It felt like someone had cut me open. It stung like nothing else. I had been sweating on the court, but it caused a different kind of perspiration. Beads of sweat suddenly covered my whole face and started dripping on the floor in front of me. It was like a strange physical reaction of my body that I had never had.

I had never been caned so I didn't really have any idea if there was a proper way of doing it. I guess I expected the person doing the caning to have mastered the skill so he knows how far to go but I'm not sure if Nikolai really cared about individual thresholds. He just believed the caning needed to be harsh and memorable. And it certainly was. After the fourth or fifth stroke, I started to get light-headed. I felt like I was getting lashed like in those images of religious zealots who are whipped until they pass out. I couldn't see the results of the cane, so I just imagined really deep welts on my skin. My legs were trembling and I began to cry again. I think the sound of my whimpering made him strike me harder so I tried to stop. Each time he lashed the cane across my bare ass, my entire body would flinch, but the more he did it, the more my mind separated itself from what was happening to my body.

Q: What do you mean?

Valentina: It was like some kind of out-of-body experience. I knew in my mind that he was whipping me viciously, but it was as if I was just watching it. The pain grew numb or subsided. It was like someone else was getting the thrashing. I zoned out. I have no idea how many he gave me or how long the whole episode lasted, but after a certain point, I began to feel like I could take it no matter what. The suffering became someone else's suffering. She deserved a beating. Her body needed to be whipped for not performing. Her ass needed to be lashed like she was a criminal. It became purely cerebral apart from my own personal feelings about it.

Q: Did you enjoy it?

Valentina: I wouldn't use the word enjoy. I once went on holiday to Odessa where there are a lot of bathhouses. After spending some time in the hot and cold baths, I paid to have, what they call in this country, "an exfoliation." This is when a specialist at the bathhouse scrubs your whole body with a kind of luffa sponge. The one she used on me, though, was incredibly rough. I felt like she was scrubbing the skin right off of my body. I mean she was, that was the point, but she scrubbed so hard it was very painful. When she stopped, I felt a great relief that she stopped. I enjoyed the fact that she stopped. But the next day, when I saw the glow of my skin in the mirror and how beautiful I looked, I was ecstatic. So in retrospect, I thought that I enjoyed the whole experience to some degree because of what it produced.

Nikolai's caning did the same thing to me but in a much more extreme way. It was the beating of this woman's body which was not completely my own. I started to hate this body during the experience in a way that I thought it should be beaten. It should be caned and receive harsh pain.

I next day, there was a sense that I had been cleansed in some way. Nikolai's disappointment in me was made real with the caning. I went out onto the court feeling refreshed. I could feel the markings on my ass. I mean I had looked at them in the mirror that night and the following morning, and they were vicious. A true thrashing of my skin.

On the court, though, I had a new sense of clarity. I saw every stroke before I made it, knew how the ball was going to bounce, anticipated the movement of my opponent…It was like a new reality. But I don't want to attribute this to Nikolai's punishment because I've seen him do such things to other women and they are never the same. They retreat and burn out. For me, the experience was separate from him. He was incidental to the pain. The creator of the pain came from within me and I was the one who let it go. I understood the meaning of the sheer agony of getting whipped like a martyr but I took it as a moment to move on and not as a moment to be held down. Not long after it happened, I left him as my coach. Maybe he knew what he did and maybe not. I'm still not sure.

Q: What do you mean?

Valentina: He was just being controlling and selfish. I think he got off on the humiliating me like that. But for me, it was a spiritual experience. It took me out of my body and made me realize that I was the one placing the limitations on my body to perform.

Q: So it just happened that one time?

Valentina: Yes. At least with him. But it changed me. Not only did I skyrocket in performance and move into the rankings of the top 100 players in the world, but I looked at the nature of physical discipline in much different terms. I made it part of my being.

Q: Were you spanked after by others?

Valentina: Yes. I get spanked at least once a week, sometimes a few times a day. I have various men who spank me. Most of them I have asked for except if I meet one of those men who just knew that I like it by the way I respond to their questions. I have met them online, in the tennis business, at parties…really anywhere. Unlike with Nikolai, I set the terms and the circumstances. I tell them where I need to get with my game and I confess to them if I haven't gotten there. There is no safe word. They cane me according to their own desires as well as in response to my reaction. If they don't believe me when I tell them that I have learned my lesson then they give me more strokes.

Q: Has this affected your personal life? Do you involve spanking in your relationships?

Valentina: At first, I kept the two quite distinct from one another. But the more I would become involved with someone, the more I was willing to tell them. It got to the point where I had to be with someone who could bridge both worlds. I wanted a man who was completely totalitarian over my life but who I could still go out to dinner with and chat about the news or a TV show. It was hard to have any kind of relationship that didn't include both. Regular men would not understand my desire to be spanked with the cane and guys with fetishes to cane typically were not able to thrive in regular dynamic social environments. It's tough.

Q: Have you found someone who can bridge the two worlds?

Valentina: No.

Savannah T., *Columbus, OH*

Q: Tell me about your experiences getting spanked.

Savannah: I first experimented with spanking in college with a male friend. We got to know each other through a mutual acquaintance. In the beginning, we started to date and ended up hooking up with each other. After having sex a number of times, he started to spank me just before we started to have sex. I was really into it but after he did it a couple of times, I asked him about it. We ended up in these long drawn-out conversations in which he would confess that he would like to get spanked himself. So we started experimenting and I would spank him. I liked it but he really liked it. I think it was what he wanted all along. Our relationship was short-lived and I didn't really keep in touch with him, but I always wondered what happened to him. When men tell me they are excited about getting spanked, I'm never sure if they desire a dominant female or are just masking their homosexual desires. I don't really care either way, but I came out of the relationship knowing that I liked to be on the receiving end rather than on the giving side.

Q: Why do you say that?

Savannah: I like the kinky urge to spank no matter what. I mean most people don't let out their true urges in a real relationship unless they are drunk or something, but there is a distinct difference between a man spanking a woman and a woman spanking a man. Men are almost always physically stronger so it is an assertion of their power over you in a physical way. For a woman to spank a man, the man must submit. The interesting thing, though, is that it is so much more complex than that. There is this play of what it means to be a man and what it means to be a woman. My father was very masculine. A tough guy. And I was a daddy's girl and an only child. I liked what my father liked– football, boxing, horseracing, hunting, and everything else that went along with proving yourself in a man's world. But I wanted to be his girl at the same time so it all got confusing when I got involved in relationships and hadn't sorted out all these mixed up feelings.

I liked the man to take charge of me and spanking was the ultimate experience of that in the bedroom. When I discovered that there are men who like to be spanked, it made me question everything about men. It was kinky in a completely different way. I really do like to spank a man's ass but it makes me feel like he is not a real man. It makes me feel like I have tested him and he cannot match up to what I idealize as a man.

Q: So after this first experience, who else?

Savannah: I got married fairly young. We were both just out of college, living in Columbus. I was really into him, I think, because he was in med school studying to be a doctor and I had just graduated from nursing school. I fantasized about us having a life together, sharing our work experiences with each other, and building a family together. It was all very definite in my mind but there was nothing concrete about it in reality. It was pure haze. After he graduated, we talked and decided to move out to California where he was going to do his residency. I think we both thought we needed the move, but in the end, we were really just looking to move away from each other. We had bought into this idea of the young couple who should move somewhere, buy a house and start a family.

The problem was that he wasn't into spanking at all. He thought I was a freak for wanting it and if I asked him to do it, he just went through the motions. He would do it occasionally in a really half-ass way, but I wanted it all the time. In the end, I asked for a divorce.

Q: A divorce? You divorced him because he wouldn't spank you?

Savannah: (laughs) Yes. I know it sounds crazy, but I had realized by that point how significant it was to me. I was working as an E.R. nurse at the time which was so intense, stressful and emotionally exhausting. When I came home, all I wanted was a total release from those moments of life and death. Having someone physically strike me brought me back to myself. Spanking made me feel alive. I also have a very high pain threshold so I need to be taken to a place that most other people don't need to be taken to. Some women get off on getting a little smack on their ass during sex. I need to be spanked hard with a man's full force to even begin to feel it. If a guy wants to spend the whole night just spanking me while we talk, that's my comfort zone.

Q: So what happened after the divorce?

Savannah: Well, I was already playing with guys toward the end. I'd meet men online who were into the fetish. We would meet and they would spank me. Sometimes we would go away for the weekend somewhere but spanking was always at the core of the connection. The spanking scene was kind of my rebound guy. It was what I resorted to when I wasn't sure about anything else.

While we were in the middle of the divorce, I moved from our house in Orange County up to L.A. We were still finalizing everything and had purchased a house together that we were waiting to sell. I just needed a new direction so I got an apartment in Hollywood and a new job.

Q: What kind of a new job?

Savannah: I started working for a plastic surgeon. He was one of the doctors-to-the-stars types. His office was in Beverly Hills and it was a total change from working in the E.R. department. With the stress of the divorce, it was actually a great change. It was really lucrative and the procedures were all very routine.

Q: How did you even find the job?

Savannah: While I was still with my husband, I became more and more interested in getting things done to my body. It wasn't really that I was unhappy with the way I looked. It was more about trying to make myself look like I felt. I longed for a physical image of myself that fit with the mixed-up conceptions I still had from being young. I wanted to look like a sexpot vixen but still be tough. I worked out six days a week and started to obsessively look at my naked body in the mirror. I just didn't want to be spanked, but I wanted to look a particular way as I got spanked. I think I became really neurotic at that point. It was like the conception of myself was breaking down but I was trying to build it up with all these changes. The only definite thing that was always good to me and real was spanking. So I thought about spankings and sought out spankings nonstop.

Q: What do you mean you wanted to still be tough?

Savannah: I don't really know. Like I said, I was much more of a daddy's girl. I felt like I disappointed him in some way with the failed marriage so I tried to pretend like I still had everything in control. I wanted to appear tough like I could withstand everything in an almost masculine way. I worked out so much that I started developing definition in my muscles. This was during the time that I got the job at the plastic surgeon's office. I had already been thinking about getting a breast enlargement and the doctor offered his employees a discount, so I just decided to do it on a whim. I was trying to reinvent myself in some way. I got hair extensions as well. A couple of months later I started competing in fitness competitions, like the kind where you show how fit you are based on how you look. It's like this world between the muscle freaks and the swimsuit contest at the beauty pageants. I was just in between anything and everybody.

Q: What do you mean?

Savannah: Between marriage and divorce, between wanting to be spanked and not getting spanked, between wanting to be this muscular tough woman and this sensitive little girl, between my old life and my new life…there was nothing definite in what I was doing. So I sought out spanking instinctually as the thing that always made me feel grounded. I randomly met someone online on a spanking site who happened to live in my neighborhood in L.A. It was really strange. Anyone who has looked for spanking connections online knows that usually the people you connect with live thousands of miles away. He lived three blocks away. Must have been telepathy or fate or something. Anyway, we met for dinner and got along well enough. I just wanted to be spanked and he took me back to my place and spanked me.

He used his hand and then his belt. He began to strike me with it really hard and he noticed right away that I wasn't really reacting. I told him that I have a really high pain tolerance, which is true. So he kept whipping me repeatedly with his belt as I was lying down on the sofa with my pants pulled down. I don't know if he was using his full force but I could tell he was trying to do it harder and harder. I could tell he was surprised that I didn't really react. I mean I liked it and it was turning me on, but I have a way of suppressing all my emotions. I really guard my feelings but getting viciously spanked puts me in a kind of zone. It hurts but it frees my thoughts in some way. It grounds me. It's like I need someone to really want to spank me hard and once they start doing it, everything is okay in my mind. It's really cerebral for me.

Q: So what happened with this new guy? Did you have a relationship with him?

Savannah: We started to. We went out several times and he would always spank me. I prodded him to see if he liked to be spanked but he didn't. I would have wanted to but I think I like it more when the guy refuses. It's just strange territory to get into. Anyway, every time he spanked me, he would always ask me all these questions about why I liked to be spanked. He would ask me if I liked to be submissive, if I liked to be controlled, if I liked to be punished…and all these other questions about it. But I would always say no. It was completely about the physical sensation of being spanked that got me off and made me feel good. I didn't want any power play with it. Just to be with a man who craves to spank his woman for the sensation of it is enough for me. I like it with sex and in kinky ways, but the simple repetition of being spanked over and over and over, day in and day out, is like this constant I want in my life more than anything else. It's hard to explain. I can psychoanalyze it but it doesn't matter. When it comes down to it, I wouldn't marry another man who didn't like to spank me all the time. That's my one rule.

Josephine E., *Brooklyn, NY*

Q: Tell me about your experiences getting spanked.

Josephine: I got spanked by my shrink. It started while I was still doing sessions with him but it continued on well after I terminated treatment under his care.

Q: How did it start?

Josephine: Someone referred him to me. I was having marital problems. I grew up in a traditional Jewish household and married a man who was a friend of the family. I was only 22 and he was the first man I had had a serious relationship with. I lost my virginity to him and I thought I wanted to spend the rest of my life with him. It turned out that I didn't know anything about him. He was a gambler, a hard drinker and didn't really follow any of the basic tenets of Judiasm. I was afraid to seek out a psychiatrist within my own community because it is very tight-knit and people talk. He would find out about it and I was afraid of how he would react. So I asked a friend from college to recommend someone. She gave me a name and told me if I was looking for someone really untraditional, he was the doctor to see.

Q: And what did really untraditional mean?

Josephine: He was a true iconoclast. He not only thought that my traditional upbringing was a total farce but he believed that anyone who believed in all the traditional institutions such as marriage, religion, family rituals, and other social norms, were simply afraid to live freely and give in to their true desires. He was young and brash. He had practiced with a group out in California but when he

155

returned to New York, he began a private practice so he could do his own thing. I believe he eventually lost his license but just kept working as an unlicensed counselor or something.

Anyway, I had no idea the type of person that my friend was referring me to. We got into a huge argument during the very first session.

Q: About what?

Josephine: I immediately began to complain about my husband and what a bad Jew he was. Dr. Fulman asked me if he was really a bad Jew or if I just thought of him in a different way than he thought of himself. He asked if my husband really cared about being a good Jew at all or if that was something I wished he was. The conversation quickly got very combative and the focus suddenly shifted to my father. My father was very strict with me and he had given me quick a few memorable spankings. Dr. Fulman asked me if it was really my husband's behavior that disturbed me or if I didn't long to do the same things he did. He asked me if I ever had any deviant sexual thoughts. I couldn't believe it. I got up and walked out.

Q: What made you do that?

Josephine: He had no right to ask me such a question. I was there to talk about my marriage and to get advice on how I can help my husband to change his behavior. What did my sexual thoughts have anything to do with that? Anyway, I told myself I would never return to see such a man and began to look for another psychiatrist. But when I went to see someone else, I was dissatisfied with him for all the opposite reasons. He told me exactly what I wanted to hear and gave me advice on how to be a good Jewish wife. If I had never gone to see Dr. Fulman, I probably just would have listened to this man and gone on with my life. Instead, I made another appointment with Dr. Fulman.

While I was waiting outside his office, I started glancing at the photos on his wall. His office was in his home so he had just transformed the foyer next to the side entrance into a waiting room. There was a photo of him in what looked like the trophy shot after he had been hunting in Africa or somewhere. He was holding up the head of a dead lion. He was crouched down with his gun strapped around his shoulder and wasn't even wearing a shirt. He just had on a pair of thick camouflage pants and heavy boots. The image looked so raw and startling. Dr. Fulman's blue eyes seemed so peaceful looking but the rest of the scene seemed so violent to me. When he suddenly opened his office door, our eyes locked and a chill went down my spine. I knew right then that there was something about him that was very attractive but particular frightening at the same time.

Q: So what happened at the session?

Josephine: He asked me why I had decided to return to see him. I told him I wasn't sure. He immediately asked me to tell him about my deviant sexual thoughts. I was, of course, shocked once again but I knew coming there that he would eventually bring it up. I just didn't expect it to be the first subject. So I started to tell him about the dreams I had started to have months before. There were many different dreams but they always seemed to be some variation of this feeling of being chased by a man who I couldn't identify. I was running away because I knew that I had done something wrong but I didn't know what it was that I did. I would wake up just as he was about to catch me.

He asked me how I felt when I woke up and I hesitated to respond. He told me to just tell him without thinking and I said I felt like I needed to be punished. He asked me what for and I told him that I didn't know. He asked me again and again but I wasn't sure. He was convinced that I was hiding something or not being forthcoming about my desires. We argued back and forth for nearly the remainder of the session. I told him more about my husband and my upbringing but it would always lead back to these longings that I could not express. Then, he glanced at the clock and told me that our time was up. We both stood up and I asked him if I should come at the same time the following week. I was shocked when he told me that it wouldn't make much sense to continue on like we had. He told me that if I couldn't speak honestly, more verbal exchanges weren't going to help me. I insisted again that I was being honest but I asked him what else I could possibly do to reveal my repressed thoughts. He glanced at me and thought for a moment. Then you know what he said?

Q: What?

Josephine: He told me he could simply punish me for my thoughts and that they might just reveal themselves. I asked him what he meant by "punish". He said, in the most casual tone, that he could spank me. I glared at him like he was joking but he was dead serious. He told me that I obviously fantasized about being punished and it was clear to him that I had returned to him for it. I couldn't believe his arrogance and his total disregard for professional distance. I told him that there was no way such a thing was permissible in his profession and I was going to file a complaint against him.

He just stared back at me and told me that I very well could and had the right to, but that I wouldn't get my spanking if I did. Can you believe he had the audacity to say that? I was just amazed that he would risk his reputation so frivolously, but that was before I learned that that was his reputation. He had no respect for the endless psychoanalyzing of every memory and thought. He thought people should act on their true impulses and focus on results. I was still standing there in total shock when he extended his hand and told me to call him if I would like another appointment. Before I could even respond, he opened the door and his next patient was already there waiting. I just rushed out of his office in a fit of anger.

Q: So what happened after that?

Josephine: I couldn't stop thinking about the conversation and about that photo of him in his office. There was something so physical and intimidating about him. He was nothing like my husband. My husband was so cerebral and neurotic. He was nothing like any man who I had ever known. There was something about him that made me feel like he was forcing himself on me. It really disturbed me. I decided I wasn't going back to see him.

Q: What did you do?

Josephine: I ended up seeing another psychiatrist and after a number of sessions, I was convinced that I wanted a divorce from my husband. My family was very shocked when I told them but I was positive that I didn't want to spend the rest of my life with him. The rabbi came to see me and it was really difficult. I finally persuaded everyone that he was a bad husband, even though he had never really done anything awful to me. I felt terribly guilty about it. It nearly made me sick every day to think about it while we went through the process.

Q: And?

Josephine: So one day, my pangs of guilty were just wreaking havoc on my state of mind and I decided to call Dr. Fulman. I told him what I was going through and asked him if I could come see him. He told me he had an opening later that day, in the early evening, and I told him that I would be there.

So, after entering his office and setting my bag on the sofa, I quickly jumped into my situation with my husband and was rattling on and on about it when he cut me short. He informed me that this is not the way he does therapy and it had been more than six weeks since we had last met. I apologized but he cut me short again. He said to me: "You're not understanding. Our agreement was for you to be punished at our next session. Your divorce is only a reaction to what you don't want. You came to me to discover what you want."

I didn't know what he fully meant but I was in such a state at that point in my life that I just said, "I'm here, aren't I?"

Q: What did he do?

Josephine: He immediately stood up and then motioned for me to stand up. He walked to his desk and took out a notebook of blank drawing paper. He had this metal tray that had wheels, like it was some kind of medical device. He put the drawing paper on it, along with a fountain pen, and wheeled it around to the back of the couch. Then he told me to put my knees up on the couch and bend over. When he said that, I realized that he was really going to do it. I had arrived in a fit of emotion but I think I knew in the back of my mind that I was going to be punished. It was almost as if I felt like I needed to be punished for being the bad Jewish wife who asks her husband for a divorce. I made some half-hearted objections to Dr. Fulman but then got into the position he told me to get into. I maintained a very formal demeanor the whole time as if this was a completely normal part of the therapeutic process.

But when he took hold of the bottom of my full-length skirt and began to lift it over my back, the reality of the situation hit me. I had never been intimate with a man outside a relationship nor revealed myself to anyone except in the darkness of a bedroom. He exposed me without any propriety. I felt so cheap. I immediately thought about what he thought about me. My impression of him was that he was a very cavalier man who probably had his fair share of woman in his travels. He must have thought I was so homely. I was wearing theses basic white panties. He put his hand on my back and ordered me to stay still. He was in control in a way that made me think he had done this before. Like it was scientific to him.

Q: And then?

Josephine: He told me he was going to spank me repeatedly and that I was to write down what I thought I was being punished for. I nodded up and down that I would. I could barely keep my composure at this point. He wasted no time. He lifted his hand and repeatedly slapped my bottom. It stung but it was more the emotional force that took over me. He must have done it a dozen times and then paused. He looked for me to write something down, but I was so engulfed in the moment that I could hardly think straight.

When he saw that I did not write anything, he said, "Very well, then. Don't worry about the transference. You believe I am personally spanking you for my own reasons. I will do it again and you will write down your thoughts. Is that understood?"

The experience was beginning to get more and more intense. He began to spank me once again but he didn't stop after the first dozen. He kept doing it and it was beginning to really hurt. My mind was racing with thoughts so I just started jotting things down. I wrote "humiliated" and "failure" and "man" and "moist" and "pain" and "wrong".

When he saw me write "wrong", he asked me if I felt the spanking was wrong or the divorce. I told him both. He mumbled something to himself and then began to smack his palm across my behind once again. The pain started to really smart but I didn't write anything else down. He kept doing it slowly for a few more moments and then said to me, "You know why you are being punished, don't you?" My mind raced for an answer but I just told him, "No." He responded to me, "Because you deserve it." I immediately said, "Yes." He asked me why I thought I deserved it.

Q: Did you think he was putting thoughts in your head?

Josephine: No, I felt like he *was* inside of my head. I did think I deserved it but I didn't know why. All these thoughts were going through my head. He spanked me again and told me to write the first thoughts that came into my head. I wrote down "memory", "father", "disappoint" and "drapes".

Q: Drapes?

Josephine: Yes, drapes. He responded in the same way. I had this memory of looking out my window one day toward the neighbor's apartment next door. It was just after I got married and we lived on the second floor of this brownstone. I noticed some movement in the window and when I peeped through the slit of the drapes, I saw that the neighbors were having sex. They didn't seem to have made any effort to cover their own drapes and the way they were having sex was really graphic. They were stark naked and the man was behind the woman doing it to her. I moved away from my own window at first but then I hid at the edge of the curtain and watched.

It was a vivid image because I couldn't hear anything but I could see the man violently thrusting his body against the woman. It was like I had to imagine the smacking sounds. The woman's face was really contorted in an expression of pleasure and she would turn back to tell the man things. I watched for at least five minutes and then I suddenly heard my front door open. It was my husband. I freaked out. All these images from the past flooded through me. It was as if all the sexual thoughts of my life flashed before my eyes.

I ran to the bathroom and closed the door. My husband called out for me. I told him I was in the bathroom and that I'd be right out. He said he was going to run back out to the store for something. I heard the door close again and I heaved a sigh of relief. I suddenly realized, though, that my underwear was wet. At first, I thought I had gone pee in my pants but I didn't. I was just really wet from being turned on by watching. I felt so guilty. I immediately took off my underwear. I got a glimpse of my bare behind in the mirror. I don't know what made me do it, but I gave myself a soft slap on my ass. I had this urge to be spanked but there was no one to do it, so I tested out doing it on myself. Once I saw it turn a little red, I did it a few more times. The more I did it, the more I felt like I wasn't spanking myself hard enough. I took out a wooden hairbrush from the cabinet and started using that. I just spanked myself furiously with it over and over as hard as I could. My cheeks were bright red but I still didn't feel like I had been punished enough. The reality of what I was doing, though, suddenly came to me. I put the hairbrush back, pulled down my skirt and went to put on a fresh pair of underwear. I felt so weird over the whole event that I had tried to completely forget it.

Q: So you told Dr. Fulman all this?

Josephine: Yes. It was such a relief to tell someone. I had kept it bottled up inside of me. After I told him, he asked me to sit back down. I confessed all these guilty feelings I had about sex. It was not just that one moment of seeing the neighbors. It was my entire life. Any time I felt desire or saw someone else just freely desiring something or someone, I had this intense negative reaction. In my mind, it was all wrong and disobedient. He asked me if I wanted more positive associations with sex and I told him that I didn't know.

I talked nearly nonstop for the rest of the session and, before I knew it, our time was up. When he told me that the session was over, the fact that he had actually spanked me in his office just moments before came back into my mind. After I had been so exposed like that to him, I felt like I could say anything. He asked me if I wanted another session and I immediately told him that I did. Then he asked me if I needed to be spanked again. I paused to think about it and I told him that I wasn't sure. We left it at that.

Q: What happened at the next session?

Josephine: We talked the whole time like a normal psychological session. He didn't even bring up the issue of the spanking and neither did I. I saw him for a number of weeks and worked on dealing with my negative views of sexual desire. I could feel it really started making a difference in my life. When I would see a couple kissing in a café or on the street, I would overtly make myself smile and let myself enjoy it. I indulged in basic pleasures like reading sex advice articles in women's magazines or eyeing store window displays of lingerie shops. I even began to experiment with touching myself at night, but that's when my old feelings started to return.

Q: What do you mean?

Josephine: I would fantasize about being bad and about getting caught watching people have sex. There were a thousand scenarios that came to me but they were always about doing something wrong and being punished for it. They always produced the strongest sexual feelings.

During one session with Dr. Fulman, I finally got the nerve to ask him if getting another spanking might do me some good. I told him about the fantasies and he asked me a number of other questions. He told me that it sounded like healthy fantasies and that he didn't believe that getting spanked in his office again would further my treatment. When he said it, he glanced at me in a particular way that made me feel like he was insinuating something. I asked him if he would be willing to spank me if I terminated treatment. He hardly had to think about it. He simply said, "Yes, I would." After the session, I settled my final payment to him and then he handed me his number written on a piece of paper. He told me that we would need to meet in a hotel room as it would not be appropriate considering his office was in his home.

Q: And did you?

Josephine: Yes, we met once a week for about two months straight. It got to be really intense. He would tie me to the bed with these brown leather straps and then would bare my bottom. I mean completely bare. He would lift my skirt and pull my panties down to the middle of my thighs. I thought he was going to use his hand but when I heard the sound of his belt moving through his belt loops on his pants, I realized what he was going to do. He would ask me questions in a similar way as he did when he gave me the one in his office, but everything felt so much more sexual. He would really whip me. Sometimes, perspiration was dripping from my forehead just from trying to endure the pain. But I loved it. It was the most illicit thing I had ever done but it seemed okay to do because it was with him. I wouldn't have done it with anyone else. I don't think I could confess to anyone else how much such a thing turns me on. By the end of each spanking session, I was so excited. And he knew it. He would simply untie the straps and tell me that he would see me at the same time the next week. After he left, I would pleasure myself to a deep orgasm.

Q: You never did anything with him?

Josephine: No. As strange as it sounds, it felt like it would be wrong or, at the very least, that I wouldn't be able to have the same intense release week after week. It was almost like a stress reliever for me as much as it was a deviant sexual thing. Unfortunately, Dr. Fulman ended up having some legal issues with all of his controversial practices and told me that he needed to take a break from the sessions. I called him a couple of times but I never heard from him again.

Heather M., *Biloxi, MS*

Q: Tell me about your experiences getting spanked.

Heather: Well, I'm from the Deep South. I got spanked for as long as I could remember just as my mom got it and her mom. It's just a way of doing things, I guess. It seems like all my boyfriends play-spanked me as well, even when we were fooling around. I don't know if that explains my fetish for it but I've had one for as long as I can remember. When I was in my early twenties, I moved to South Carolina for a job. I really didn't want to leave Mississippi but the job paid really well and I was single. I ended up not really liking the job though, and was pretty miserable. I had kept in touch with some of my friends from home as well as my good friends from college. I started reaching out to them more just because I was going crazy. Some of them still lived in Mississippi but others were living throughout the South. I had been in a sorority with my friends in college but I was closer to the friends I had grown up with. Anyway, some of us met up for a weekend in Mobile, Alabama just to get away and we had this long drunken conversation about getting spanked. This was where it all started.

Q: What started?

Heather: The Southern Spanked Girls Social Club. We had come up with a bunch of other names, ones that were more local or personal or private, but we figured we should just keep it simple. It was really straight to the point—we were girls from the South who liked to be spanked. I had a tighter bond, as far as spanking, with the girls with who I had been in the sorority. We went through the whole hazing ritual together and had all been paddled by the older members. We felt like we knew how to do things as far as making the rules of the organization. My friends from home, though, disagreed. Not only had many of them not even gone to college, but some of them grew up in more rural parts where the whippings could get brutal. So, even though we were all in agreement about why we wanted such a club, there was a disagreement about the direction of it. The sorority girls wanted it be about hazing the other girls and prepping each other for marriage. The Deep South girls wanted it to about pure discipline and doing what you are told.

Q: So how did this work out? Did you meet to discuss these things?

Heather: Yes, we had our first informal meeting in Mobile. When I say informal, I mean informal. We just made an agreement before we went out to the bars that any girl who didn't up in man's room getting her ass spanked would be whipped by the whole group the following day. It was pretty simple. The first night, we were all so kinky and drunk that we each come back the next morning with beaten butts. We each had to show it off to the other members as proof. Some girls were already showing marks while others had to convince us that they had really gotten it.

But, the next night, things went awry. I ended up meeting this guy, Jayden, who I thought was not only really attractive but someone who I could see myself having a relationship with. So, at the end of the night, we just gave each other a kiss and went home.

But when I got back to the vacation house we were all sharing and told them what happened, all hell broke loose. My friends from school understood that I had met someone, but my friends from home didn't care about anything but the rules. I hadn't been spanked so I would get it the next day. We argued about it for a while and then just went to bed.

Q: And what happened the next day?

Heather: I woke up to the feeling of the sheets being ripped off of my body. Two of my good friends from home, Daisy and Hallie, were standing above me on the bed. I looked up at them in shock. My other friend, Scarlett, was standing at the edge of the bed with a huge wooden paddle. I knew what was coming but I freaked out anyway and tried to get away. There was a struggle but I was completely out-womaned. They pinned me down and turned me over. They held my head down on the bed and my arms to my sides so that only my butt was still upright. Scarlett placed the paddle against my skin so I knew what was coming. It was such as strange moment because I knew how they felt and I believed in that, but at the same time I was on the side of my sorority friends who were more open-minded. They understood that I might have met someone special but my friends from home just knew that rules were rules.

When Scarlett whipped the huge paddle across my butt, my whole body jerked forward. It had been some time since I got it. I had been spanked recently but getting the thick piece of wood smacked across your ass is entirely another thing. It thuds against the meat of your cheeks and you know it's going to leave marks. I mean I have given them and I have taken them, but the whole ritual of striking someone's posterior with a piece of wood seems kind of medieval. And it hurts like hell. It's like getting assaulted on your butt. Scarlett does a good job of swinging the paddle, too, so she doesn't leave any place untouched. She makes sure you know you've been paddled. You feel it and see it the next day. While you are getting it, though, you just try and zone out. All the other girls are shouting and saying things about you, but you just want it to be over. Afterward, the thought of it seems kind of kinky but only after you are finished taking your whippings.

Q: So what happened with this guy you met?

Heather: We met again the next night. Jayden was from Mississippi as well. That's how our conversation began. He was really well-educated, though. He came from an old Southern family and his great-grandfather had donated so much money to Ole Miss that there was a building named after him. I was a little afraid of telling him about my spanking fetish, not to mention my membership in such a club. On our first date, while all my friends were out at the bars, we went out to dinner. It was unbelievably romantic and we were totally engrossed in each other's lives. We agreed on certain things, had fierce debates on other things and were ready to rip each other's clothes off on the spot. But he was very much the southern gentleman type. At the end of the night, he simply took me home and gave me a couple of deep-tongued kisses.

The next morning, I got a second paddling from my friends from home. They demanded to know why he hadn't spanked me and why I hadn't brought up the fact that I liked to be spanked. They thought that either he wasn't right for me or that I wasn't being fully honest with him. In any case, they gave me a fierce paddling on the bed. The next day my butt was in pain and there were even a few black and blue marks from the spanking.

Q: But it was worth it?

Heather: Definitely. But they were also right in a way. I hadn't mentioned how much I liked and needed to be spanked. I also wondered if he was too uptight to want a girlfriend, or wife, who he thought of as a woman who needed to be spanked. For me, it was a sign of desire and possession and love all mixed together. If a man wasn't ready to get physical with his woman in certain ways, then he didn't really care enough about her to pursue a long-term relationship. Those were just my beliefs. But I didn't really know him well enough at all to say one way or the other.

When I got back to South Carolina, we began to talk nonstop. We were really into each other and were both looking for a serious relationship. The only problem was that we lived hundreds of miles away from each other. I started to go visit him on weekends as much as I could but it was difficult.

Q: Did you finally tell him about your desire to be spanked?

Heather: No. Things were going so well and he seemed so vanilla and traditional that I was scared that he would think I was some kind of a freak. I still, though, got together with my friends from the spanking club. A couple of them lived near me and we would go out. Well, like the third time we went out, one of them invited this group of guys who she knew from school. She had told them that we all liked to get spanked but she didn't tell me that she had told them. I guess she thought I wouldn't come if I knew that they knew because I had a serious boyfriend. So, I ended up kind of clicking with this one guy, Noah. He was the kind of guy who was really forward and kept touching me the whole time we were talking. I told him I was seeing someone so I thought he understood, but my two friends kept looking over at us and laughing.

So towards the end of the night, I told everyone that I was going to head home. So this guy says he'll walk me to my car. I just shrugged and said fine. My friend knew his friends so I wasn't worried. So we walked to my car which was parked behind the place far back in the lot. When we got to it, I was about to turn to thank him for escorting me when he suddenly grabbed me and swatted me hard on the butt. I kind of laughed and then asked him what that was for. He just put his hand on my waist and told me to turn around and put my hands on my car. My mind started racing trying to figure everything out while I glanced to make sure there was no one else in the parking lot. I didn't know what to do. I didn't think I had mentioned to him that I liked to be spanked, but I wasn't sure.

I should have just told him that I needed to go but I didn't. I turned around and hesitantly lifted my hands to the side of my car. He immediately started spanking me over my skirt and I just stood there and let him. It's like my Achilles heel. As soon as I feel the sensation of someone slapping my ass, I go into this zone where everything else seems to fade into the background. So after he gives me a half dozen of them, he asks me, "I thought you had a boyfriend?"

Q: What did you say?

Heather: I told him that I did and he tells me that I deserve to be spanked then for being so naughty. I looked back at him, started to take my hands down and told him I needed to go. He grabbed a hold of one of my wrists, placed it back on the car and told me: "Not before you get a good, hard spanking." I felt him lift up my skirt and my heart jumped. I looked back again to make sure there was no one else in the parking lot. He began to spank me repeatedly over my underwear. Some of his slaps struck against my bare skin which sent waves of pleasure through my body. I thought that he had just decided to grab me and spank me. I always fantasize about that but it never happens. I had no idea that my friends had told him.

He spanked me over and over in really fast, hard strokes. I squirmed to get away from it but he could tell that I was into it. We both heard the sound of voices and looked to see a group of people on the other side of the lot walking to their car. I thought he was going to stop but he didn't. He told me to turn my face in their direction and smile so they knew I was enjoying it and not getting attacked. I protested for him to just wait until they were gone but he just kept spanking me. I didn't know what to do so I just turned and laughed. I glanced over at the group of people and they were looking at us and smiling. Noah had casually slipped my underwear between my cheeks and was spanking my bare ass at this point. He kept doing it until the group of people got in their car and drove away. Finally, he stopped. I think my face must have been as red from embarrassment as my butt was red from the spanking. I asked him how he knew I would let him spank me and he confessed to me that my friends had told him. I couldn't believe it. I almost wished he hadn't told me as it was so exhilarating to think that he just did it because I deserved it.

Q: What happened after that?

Heather: We talked briefly before I left. He asked me if my boyfriend spanked me and I told him that he didn't. I explained the situation to him. He replied that, in that case, he would spank me every week until I confessed to him. I laughed, thinking he was joking, and told him no. He asked me if Monday night worked for me. I told him no again. He told me to give him my phone number. I hesitated for a moment and then just gave it to him. I didn't know what I was going to do, but at least it got me into my car and out of there. The first thing I did when I got home was drop my purse, fall on the couch and touch myself. I had such an intense orgasm.

Q: So what did you do after that night?

Heather: Uhhmm, well, to make a long story short, I started to stop by his place on the way home from work on Monday to get spanked. At first, I told myself that I would just do it once but it quickly became a regular thing. It became this ritual in my schedule. I would drive to his place and ring his doorbell. When he opened the door, he already had a chair placed in the center of his living room. Each time, right after he opened the door, he would just swat me and order me to get over the chair like he was really angry with me. It made my kinky insides swoon in pleasure. I hadn't done anything new but he was really good at pretending to be furious at me, like it was the first time I was disobedient over and over again.

I would bend over the chair and, depending on what I was wearing, would flip up my skirt or pull down my pants. Then he would just rip my panties down to my ankles in a quick, forceful motion. It sent chills through me. Usually, he would start spanking me right away but sometimes he would leave me like that for a while until he was ready to discipline me. Sometimes he would be in the middle of doing something when I arrived so he would make me wait. One time, he was on the phone talking business with someone and I remained bent over exposed for like half an hour. It made me so wet by the time I got it, I can't even tell you. When he started spanking me, he would demand to know if I had told my boyfriend and I, of course, would confess that I hadn't. He would scold me over and over for being dishonest, telling me I deserved to get spanked like a naughty girl and that we was going to whip me each and every time until I learned my lesson. It was so hot.

Q: Did you ever learn your lesson?

Heather: No. I was still going back and forth nearly every weekend to see Jayden in Oxford where he lived. At first, I was totally guilty when I saw him but I slowly got used to it. It was like my dirty little secret. Plus, as I let more and more time pass, it became harder and harder for me to get the nerve to tell him. Not only did I now have to confess to him that I had a spanking fetish but I had to tell him that some random guy was spanking me every week for not telling him. The lie got too big to unravel. I think the distance made it easier as well to separate the two worlds.

One time, though, he noticed that I had marks on my ass. Usually, because Noah spanked me on Monday and I wouldn't see Jayden until Friday, there was time for it to recover and I would arrive in Oxford with a fresh white butt. After one especially harsh session with the paddle, though, there were still marks. I didn't realize it until Jayden saw them when I was getting dressed. I told him that I had fallen in the shower. I made sure to check myself after that and to ask Noah to not be too brutal.

Q: So how long did this last?

Heather: Nearly a year. I can't believe it now that I think back about it. It seemed like he spanked me in every which way possible. With his hand, his belt, various paddles and straps, a ruler…many other implements. He tried to get me to have a relationship beyond the spanking but I absolutely refused. The irony was that I ended up breaking up with Jayden but still kept going to see Noah for a couple months after I did. I didn't even tell him. I just kept confessing my misdeeds and he always found new ways to scold me. After a while, though, it no longer felt the same. In any case, it didn't matter because I ended up moving back to Mississippi. The sessions with Noah ended and Jayden never found out about any of it before we broke up.

Q: And now?

Heather: Now? Well, I'm currently single and am not being spanked by anyone either. I hope I'll meet someone who I feel like I can share both worlds with but I kind of liked having that dirty secret as well. I don't know. I wouldn't want to truly jeopardize any relationship because of my need to be spanked but I'm really not sure I could ever be with someone in a serious relationship without having that need fulfilled in some way. I guess time will tell. We still have our Southern Spanked Girls Social Club, though. It's actually grown as the years have gone on. There are regular meetings and we have this private website that you have to put in a password to see. Members post notices about meetings and who's gotten married. We still go on our annual vacation to Mobile. I'm sure you could write a whole book about just some of the things that happen there.

Leanne A., *Atlanta, GA*

Q: Tell me about your experiences getting spanked.

Leanne: I've always liked to get spanked during sex but I met this one guy who was really into it. He was also the first black guy I've ever been with so it was quite a novel fling for me. I had just broken up with a boyfriend who I had been seeing for a couple of years and I really wasn't looking for anything serious. I was out at a club with some of my girlfriends and we were out to let loose. The place was known for its hip-hop scene and there was always a very strong interracial mix there. So, we were out on the dance floor and this group of black guys started mixing in with us. It was obvious that we were all fairly drunk so the guys assumed that we were there to get it on. They weren't really our types. They weren't all thugged-out but they were definitely going for that hardcore look even though they were fairly educated.

We were all dancing and it was really crowded on the floor. It wasn't until the man I was dancing with started groping me that I really took a good look at him. Before that, it was just like this swarm of men that came up to us and it didn't seem like any one of them picked out any one of us. When his hands moved down to the curve of my ass, though, I looked up to check him out. He had this slick athletic look to him and I definitely felt the attraction, but like I said, I had never been with a black guy so it was very new and strange for me. I think I wanted him to look very forbidden or something. He was wearing these dark blue jeans but you could see his bright white boxers peeping above the waist when he adjusted his shirt. For some reason, it was such a turn-on.

Anyway, he was practically fondling me on the dance floor as he grinded his body against mine. I looked over at one of my friends and the guy she was with was practically doing the same thing. We just smiled at each other. We were just in the mood to get wild. Suddenly, though, he gave me a quick slap on my ass. I looked up at him in surprise but he just glared down at me like it was nothing and went on dancing.

Q: So what happened?

Leanne: We danced for a while longer and then moved to the lounge area to get some drinks. My friends aren't necessarily prudish but they definitely aren't the type to really go wild outside of a certain comfort zone. We all knew we were just having a good time and then we'd go home. The guy I was dancing with, Kayron, asked me for my number. I resisted at first but he was really persistent, and I was really drunk, so I just gave it to him. We were trying to talk to each other but the music was so loud we had to shout-talk into each other's ear. But he started talking really dirty to me, telling me outright that he was going to hold me down and "smack the white right off of my ass." He said a lot of other kinky things but I especially remember that one. He was turning me on in the heat of the moment but I didn't expect it to really go past that.

As it got late, my friends and I agreed that we were really to leave. I had to pry Kayron's hands off of me. I swear he was ready to fuck me right in the club. We went outside and hailed a couple of taxis. I was going in a different direction than my friends so I just took my own cab. As it was pulling away from the curb, I looked out the window and Kayron was standing outside the club giving me this knowing smile. He casually held up his phone and pointed to it in this really calm, collected way. It was like he just assumed he was going to have me.

Q: Did he?

Leanne: He called me a couple of minutes later and asked me why I left alone. I told him that I lived in a different part of town and he asked me where. I don't know why but I was afraid to tell him. I asked him, instead, where he lived. He told me he had a house that he shared with a couple of friends. It was in a decent neighborhood. I don't know if I was being racist but I was kind of surprised. Then he told me to meet him there in 15 minutes. I laughed and told him that I was on my way home. He told me that I didn't need to worry about what my friends thought anymore because they were gone. I didn't know what to say. I suddenly realized that I *was* thinking about what they thought when I was talking to him. I mean we all were, but it was unexpectedly very different now that we were talking on the phone. It felt like I was now in my own private world.

He told me again to meet him at his place and then started talking dirty to me once more. Now I started to get horny but at the same time, I was worried about going to a total stranger's house. I told him to take a picture of his license and send it to me. I figured that at least I would know who he was and know that he wouldn't send it if he really intended to do any harm to me. He sent it to me right away. His name was really Kayron, he really lived where he said he did and he was really six foot two and 185 pounds. He called me right back and asked me if I was coming. I had never done anything like this but it felt so exhilarating. At any other time in my life I don't think I would have done it, but I was just feeling like I needed to really live fully in the moment. So I told him yes.

Q: What happened?

Leanne: When I got to his place, he was already there. I rang the doorbell and he opened the door right away. He had that same look on his face as he did when I saw him outside the club from the taxi. When I walked in, his two other friends from the club were sitting in the living room with the lights out, watching music videos on this huge plasma TV. One of them asked me where my friends were and I didn't know what to say. Kayron told them that they "gots no skills" and it was past their bedtime. Then, right in front of them, he smacked my ass and wrapped his arm around me from behind. I felt like such a slut. His friends were watching while he fondled me and kissed me on the neck. He slapped my ass again and started whispering dirty things in my ear. I think he knew how embarrassed it made me feel but that I liked it deep down. No one's ever treated me like that. It felt a bit degrading but it felt more forbidden that I was letting him do it.

He led me upstairs to his room and closed the door. He immediately took hold of me and kissed me really deeply. I tried to kiss him back but it was more like he was engorging me with his thick tongue. He spanked my ass again and I started to realize how much he liked to spank. He lifted my dress up and did it a few more times. He asked me if I liked that and I told him yes. Then he asked me again and again as he spanked it harder and harder, and I told him yes again and again. He reached both of his hands underneath my dress and roughly groped my bare cheeks. He kept telling me how attracted he was to my body over and over. I've never been with anyone who desired me so overtly. He asked me if I had ever been with a black man before and I confessed that I hadn't.

He started to talk really dirty to me. He told me he was going to "make that white cunt his" and that he was going to "beat the pussy up." Then he asks me in a whisper in my ear: "You want to be my little white bitch?" I had no idea what to say. It felt humiliating but also really kinky and taboo. I laughed at first, but then he slid his hand up the front of my dress, started to fondle me underneath my panties and asked me the question again. After the fourth or fifth time he asked, as my breathing grew deeper and the pleasure began to radiate through me, I told him yes.

Q: It turned you on because he was black?

Leanne: That was part of it but also because the kind of black guy he was. I've worked with all kinds of black men but he was definitely not like them. It was the way he treated me. Maybe it was some white girl's fantasy of a black gangster. I don't know. He just spanked me like I was his piece of meat or something. It was a side of men I had never seen. Even though the rational part of me knew it was kind of degrading, it felt honest. And I was just ridiculously turned on by it all. It was exhilarating.

The whole thing moved forward in these flashes of physicality mixed with the raw, dirty way he was speaking to me. While we were still standing, he would tell me to spread my legs while he touched me. He turned me around, started to spank my ass, and then told me to bend over and touch the floor. I've never had a guy make me do that. I held my legs straight and spread, with my palms spread out on the carpeted floor, while he spanked me over and over. He kept telling me that I was "a naughty little freak." I have never thought of myself like that but he was making me feel like I was.

He pulled me back up and started to take off my dress. He said, "Strip down, bitch." It shouldn't have turned me on but it did. I helped to take off my dress and then quickly removed my bra and underwear. When I looked up, he was nearly naked himself. His body looked like he spent all day at the gym—broad chest, perfect abs and those muscular curves that wrapped around the side of his waist toward his groin. I was still eyeing his body when he grabbed me and pushed me onto his bed face-first. I was only on my hands and knees for a split second, though, when he grabbed my arms and pulled them behind me. I turned my head to the side as it hit the mattress. He told me to "get that ass in the air" as he spanked each of my cheeks repeatedly until I arched my back and pushed my butt out. He suddenly smacked me on my inner thigh and told me to "spread 'em." Everything he said was so blunt. When he walked over to get protection, he just looked at me and smiled. He stood there slowly prepping himself like he had all the time in the world. He just eyed his body and got a little nervous because he had a really huge cock.

Q: So was the spanking just a minor part of the experience?

Leanne: No. It was definitely a major part. I mean it was part of his whole demeanor. I've been spanked as foreplay before but never so hard and in such an unashamed manner. He was very physical but the spanking really made it intense. At moments, I was a little afraid but the fear was sexual. The more he did it, the more I became uninhibited to it all. As he was getting himself ready, he was staring at me as I waited in that obscene sexual position with my head on the bed, my arms behind my back and my ass pushed up in the air. He asked me, "Are you my little white bitch?" I smiled and then laughed. I had somewhat gotten used to the situation and I finally had the nerve to ask him if he always spoke to women like that.

When I said it, though, the smile slowly evaporated from his face. Instead of answering me, he strutted over to me, kneeled behind me and started spanking me again. He did it several times even harder than before. My ass was already tingling and sensitive, and each one hurt even more. He bent down to me and asked me again if I was his little white bitch. I started to gasp and breathe in and out from the spanking, but he kept doing it and kept asking me. Finally, I told him, yes, but he told me to say it. When I heard myself say, "I'm your little white bitch," it took me to a whole other level of submitting to the moment. I actually began to really feel like I was.

He kneeled behind me and eased himself into me ever so slowly. It took several minutes for me to relax enough to really take his cock all the way in me, but even after I felt it push as deep as it would go, I realized that he had not put the full length of it inside of me. I was used to feeling the touch of a guy's body when I got it from behind but I never felt his. It was just like he was poking me with it. It was hard to get used to the feeling and it was only after he started spanking me again that the pleasure came. I needed that sense of physical contact.

He started to tell me again how much he desired me, how good that "tight white cunt" felt, how "tasty" I looked beneath him, and all kinds of other things. He took hold of my arms with one of his hands and continued to spank me with the other. I tried to relax but he kept ordering me to "squeeze that black cock" and would moan when I did. He suddenly took one of my hands and put it between my thighs. I started to rub my clit back and forth as he spanked me harder and harder while he fucked me deeper and deeper. He said, "Let me hear you cum, bitch. Let me hear you cum." I was already so turned on that it didn't take long for me to reach an orgasm. It was so intense. The nonstop spanking, his dirty talk, the engorging feeling of his cock in me, me rubbing my clit – it all built up to this insane intensity. I was moaning and cursing and screaming. It was definitely one of the most powerful orgasms I have ever had. I don't even know when he came because I was so engrossed in my own pleasure. It was only after I climaxed that I realized he had come and his body was suddenly resting on top of me and we were both flat on the bed in a mess of sweat and exhaustion.

Q: And after?

Leanne: After? You mean after I left?

Q: You left right away?

Leanne: Yeah, pretty much. I mean after I went to the bathroom and cleaned up. I looked at my ass in the mirror and I couldn't believe how red it was next to the rest of my white skin. I could see how it would turn someone on. It turned me on and it was my body. I even looked at it again and again after I got home.

Q: Did you see him again?

Leanne: No. It was definitely a one-night stand. He called me a couple of times after that but I never returned his call. I don't think it would have been as good and, in retrospect, I honestly couldn't even believe that I did it. I never told any of my friends about it. I just fantasize about it over and over in my mind.

Basima F., *Kuwait City, Kuwait*

Q: Tell me about your experiences getting spanked.

Basima: It's a long story. When I first started getting it, I hated it. Basically, my ex-husband would cane me for what he thought were my disobedient actions. I was fairly young when I married but it was totally normal by Kuwaiti standards. It was kind of an arranged marriage but I thought I was completely in love with him at the time. He was from a very prominent family in Dubai and my father knew his father. Introductions were made, we went out several times and things quickly grew serious. I didn't have any experience in relationships, or with men, and I completely romanticized him. I wanted to see him as this strong but sensitive man who was also very modern in his views. After we got married, though, I quickly realized how traditional he was. It was as if he had told me all the things he told me just to get me to marry him. Once we moved into our new house in Dubai, I was practically forbidden to ever leave without him. I don't know if it was the influence of his family who were very well-known in the city and very old-fashioned, but he told me that he didn't think it was appropriate for me to be out of the house without him. He quickly found out, though, that I had a very rebellious nature and wasn't used to being kept like a prisoner.

Q: What did you do?

Basima: At first, I just argued with him repeatedly. Sometimes it was about going out but other times we fought over politics or sex. We were two very different individuals once the excitement of being young and in love wore off. The fighting went on for several months until one day I decided to outright disobey him and go out shopping

185

without telling him. I spent the whole afternoon buying thousands of dollars worth of clothes at the most expensive new stores in the city. I even bought all this lingerie that I knew he would disapprove of. It was like I wanted to just go wild and I didn't care. It was all with his credit card as well. I didn't have a job at the time and I only received a moderate allowance from my father. It felt, though, like I had broken out of jail. Even though we had only been married for less than a year, I suddenly realized how different my life had become. I had almost grown accustomed to living hidden in that house. When I returned that evening, though, everything erupted. I'll never forget it.

Q: What happened?

Basima: The moment I walked into the door, my husband started yelling at me. He told me that he had been looking for me for hours and he was furious that I would just go off like that. When he saw all the clothes that I had bought, he went crazy. He grabbed one of the bags and threw it across the room. He was absolutely enraged and it was the first time that I was actually scared of him. I had never seen him like that. He was always very strong-willed from the first moment we met, but I had never experienced it directed at me in such a negative way. He ordered me to go wait for him in the bedroom. He told me that I had crossed a line and that I needed to be punished. At the time, I was outraged that he would try to treat me like that. I felt like a naughty child and I was about to protest, but I didn't.

He was so angry and I was really confused. This strange mixture of emotions flooded through me. On the surface, I didn't think I had done anything wrong, but deep down I felt guilty. I had been raised to be a good loyal Arab woman and there was suddenly a sense in me that I had really been a bad wife. I think I was just transferring my own mixed feelings toward my father onto him. I don't know. While I sat on the bed and waited for him, a million thoughts were going through my head. I didn't really know what he meant by getting punished. I thought he was going to take away the few privileges I had at the time, but I didn't understand why he would make me wait in the bedroom for him.

When he opened the door, he had two of the servants with him. I immediately saw the cane in his hand. My heart began to beat wildly. I knew that many women were caned by their husbands, but that was mostly in fundamentalist countries such as Saudi Arabia. I had never in my wildest imagination expected a man like my husband to do such a thing. I quickly stood up and made a move toward the bathroom. One of the servants raced to block the doorway and before I knew it, each one of them had a hold of me. I began to shout at my husband but he simply ignored me and ordered the servants to hold me over the end of the bed. I struggled to get away but they were way too strong. They held me down by the wrists even though I was trying to squirm away.

My husband told me that I was going to receive 20 lashes and that if I didn't stop struggling, that he would give me 40. At first, I still tried to struggle away from the servants but my husband began to loudly scold me. He chastised me for being a bad wife and being so disrespectful to him. He asked me what people who knew him would have thought if they saw me buying lingerie by myself. I suddenly felt really humiliated even though I shouldn't have been. The fact that he was scolding me in front of the servants made it even worse. It was as if everyone recognized that I had been a bad woman except me. I stopped struggling and just submitted to everything after that. The tears started streaming down my face even before the first lash. The whole experience felt like it lasted an eternity.

Q: How exactly did he do it?

Basima: He ordered one of the servants to lift up my dress. I think he wanted me to feel the humiliation as much as the pain. To be bared by my own servant was like being reduced to nothing more than an object. I was so ashamed. He took hold of the bottom of my dress and methodically lifted it up over my back. I just stared straight ahead at that point. I didn't even want to look at either of the servants. My husband stood behind me and began to lecture me about the proper behavior of a wife and so on. I could sense him walking back and forth as he spoke. It seemed like he wanted me to really feel the embarrassment. Finally, his hands grasped the sides of my underwear and he pulled them down to my ankles. The blood rushed to my face from the sheer humiliation. I could see the tears dropping from my eyes onto the brightly colored bedspread. My body was trembling in expectation.

When he touched the hard cane against my bare skin, I flinched. I had never felt so powerless to the will of someone else like that. I was almost eager for him to strike it against me just to get it over with. The anticipation was the worst. When he held the cane flush against my bare backside, it made me feel calm in a weird way. I don't know why. Then he lifted it off of me and a split second later brought it down hard against my bare skin. My senses were so wound up that it was as if time slowed down and I could hear and feel everything. I heard the whisping sound of the cane flying through the air and I felt the sharp sting across the whole width of my body. The sound of it striking my flesh seemed to linger in the room for a few seconds. I think I was imagining the servants listening to it over and over.

After the first few lashes, I was actually relieved. Waiting in that position was more painful for me than the actual sting of the cane. The remainder of the lashes hurt but by that time I had already submitted to everything. I even felt, in some sense at that point, that I deserved to be punished for my actions. It was an overwhelming experience. I had nothing to compare it to. I never expected my husband to treat me in such a way. It was almost barbaric. It took me to places inside of myself that I didn't even know existed.

Q: What happened after that?

Basima: After the final lash, the servants let go of me and everyone left the room. I fell on the bed and began to really cry. I had all these mixed feelings and was just trying to think straight. Once I was alone, without the fear and humiliation, I started to really gain perspective about what had happened. I knew that deep down I didn't think I had really deserved to be punished, much less disciplined in such a humiliating way. I didn't know how I could ever be with my husband after that, but the whole event was so fresh that I didn't really know how to react. I stayed in bed and fell asleep a few hours later. The next morning, I found out my husband had left for a few days. I avoided even talking to the servants. I felt so embarrassed even looking at them, knowing that they had witnessed me like that. All I did while he was gone was sleep and eat.

I told myself I was going to leave him but I had no idea what that meant. I had only been married a short time and was still getting used to it. I knew that if I told my family that I wanted a divorce, they would think I was crazy and would be totally against it. I didn't personally know anyone who was divorced but society then generally viewed divorced women as some kind of whores.

Q: What did you do?

Basima: When my husband returned a few days later, he acted like everything was normal. It was almost as if the caning had never happened and he was just coming back from a business trip. In my mind, though, nothing was the same. He had fundamentally changed the nature of our relationship. I knew that I would never have any true sense of freedom with him. He would always view me as his woman as if I was his personal property. I was to know my place or he would let me know it.

I didn't have the will, though, at that point to leave him. I felt like I couldn't even tell my family what had happened. The only person I told was a good friend of mine and she didn't really have any answers for me. I still had strong feelings for my husband but my nature was naturally independent and rebellious.

Time passed and I didn't act. It was almost like I validated the punishment by not saying or doing anything about it. The event lingered in my mind for weeks and weeks. It put into perspective everything in my life. I saw myself and my family in a stark new light. I had always thought of my father as this very protective figure but now I realized that it wasn't so simple. He viewed me as his girl. In a sense, he owned me and he saw it as his responsibility to set me up in a suitable marriage. I felt like he had brought me up to be dependent on him taking care of me so it was what I would look for in a man. I suddenly got the sense that he had traded me to my husband in return for the benefit of having a well-married daughter. I had a very good relationship with my father but I now felt like an animal that had been sold off. And I had nowhere to go.

Q: So you stayed in the marriage?

Basima: For the short term, yes. It seemed like the best thing was to see if things changed. But it just wasn't in me. I think I have a split personality. I wanted to please everyone and be the good wife, but my natural emotional state is just too volatile. There's a part of me that refuses to be told what to do no matter what. I need to feel free and unconstrained.

So despite my attempts at making the relationship work, we had more arguments. Eventually, I acted out again and he caned me again. He did it several more times. Finally, one weekend I left and took a flight back to Kuwait. I told my family that I wanted a divorce. I had some kind of a mental breakdown. They all thought I was crazy. I didn't tell anyone about the canings. I just told them that my husband was abusive and I was not ever going back to him.

Q: What did they say?

Basima: At first, they thought I was nuts. They thought I had some mental problems. My father asked me to go see a psychiatrist and I did. It helped to talk about it but I still had no intention of going back to him. My father eventually spoke with his father and a divorce was granted. I was so relieved. I moved back into my parents' house and it was like returning to childhood. I tried to pretend like the whole thing didn't happen.

Q: And after?

Basima: I spent the next couple of years being a single divorced woman in Kuwait. I started my own business selling high-end cosmetics from Europe and the U.S. but it was with my father's money. So I was an independent woman but still totally dependent on him. There are so few options for a woman in that part of the world. I have a group of friends who have a similar outlook but it seems like all we do is meet for drinks at some hip new bar in Kuwait City and complain. Nobody ever does anything. I was still a divorced woman who was totally conflicted.

Q: Conflicted?

Basima: Yes. I wanted to be married again but my emotions were all mixed up. I had to be independent but I started having more and more fantasies of being a kept woman. I imagined myself as being taken and held captive against my consent. It was my way of dealing with what I wanted. I fantasized about a man just taking me against my will and caning me for every little offense. It was like I wanted both the freedom and the captivity. I no longer wanted to just be totally free and alone. I wanted to be the personal property of a man. It was like I turned around everything I had rebelled against. I wanted a man to make me his and give me lashings every time I tried to escape. I started to fantasize about it constantly. I didn't want the kind of relationship I had had with my ex-husband. I wanted a man who was just as aware of the two worlds as I was. He would punish me and keep me locked up as much for me as himself.

Q: So what did you do?

Basima: I dated a number of men but they were never the type. I was afraid to confess my desires. I started to travel a lot for business but really I just wanted to meet European and American men who were more open-minded. I had a handful of affairs with men over a couple of years. Outside of my own world, I felt like I could be more myself. I began to explore my sexuality more by finding kinky things online and then trying them in person. I would ask men to tie me up, to spank me, to take me roughly, to force themselves on me and all sorts of other things. I had some really great sex. It was my personal awakening to the darker world of sensuality. It was a really exhilarating time in my life. I'll always savor it. But as time passed, I wasn't meeting any men who I would want to spend the rest of my life with. I grew depressed again and started to recede into my own world. I thought it was all hopeless until I met Kiran.

Q: Who is Kiran?

Basima: Kiran was stationed in Kuwait when I met him randomly out one night at a bar. I don't want to say too much, but at the time he was an American soldier who was in an elite unit in the Army. He is black and he grew up with a father who had converted to Islam so he had some understanding of the religion. When we met, he made sure to point that out as if it would win my respect or something. I appreciated that he knew the basic tenets of the religion but he had no idea about the suppressive nature of it when it is used in the way it is used by most men. But that's not really made me attracted to him.

Q: What attracted you to him then?

Basima: First, his body. He looked like he just walked off the battle fight. He wasn't just muscular but he had this battle-ready stature. Relaxed but ready to kill. It was so sexy. And when we started talking, sparks just flew. I combated everything he said but he loved to argue with me. He seemed to be invigorated by the fact that I had a whole battalion of strong opinions, not only as proof I was intelligent but because he wanted to defeat my arguments. It was such a turn-on. I would go on and on and on about how I thought I was right about something and he would keep coming back with something else. Finally, he asked me about my personal life. He wanted to know why such a woman as myself wasn't married and what I was doing out at a bar talking to an American soldier at one in the morning.

Q: What did you say?

Basima: Well, I was a little bit drunk so I had the courage to say something I probably wouldn't have said otherwise. I told him that I was looking for a man who knew what to give me. He asked what I meant by that. I told him I needed a man with an open mind and a strong hand. He glanced at me briefly and our eyes locked. I could tell that he knew what I meant at the same time he wasn't sure if I was really saying what I was saying. So, I leaned over and whispered in his ear, "If you think I need to a few lashings, I probably do." I can't believe I said it. He leaned his head back, took a hard look at me and I turned away with a blush on my face. He wrapped his hand around me and then dug his fingers into the edge of my backside. He started to interrogate me after that and I confessed everything that I liked. It was getting late, though, and I was still living at home with my parents and needed to go.

The next day, we met at a hotel. I couldn't believe it. He brought a cane. He said he bought it at a local market on his way there. He told me that the vendor told him it was made for disciplinary purposes. I laughed because I knew he was just making that up. He told me to turn around and bare my ass. He told me that I had "mouthed off" to him the night before. He told me that I needed to "get whipped". He used all these American expressions that sounded so sexy despite the fact that he was telling me he was going to cane me. I protested that he didn't have any right to speak to me like that. He told me to bend over. I said no. He pushed me down on the bed. I struggled against him and he grabbed me around the waist. I told him I would scream and he said, "Yes, you will." It was so intense. He forced me to bend over, ripped my panties down at the same moment he pulled up my dress and just started lashing me. I stopped struggling right away and planted my hands on the bed. He knew what I wanted and I knew what I wanted.

He whipped the cane across my bare skin really hard. It felt much more forceful than any man had done it but it was so good. The more he enflamed my skin, the more I got turned on. He just kept lashing me over and over and over. Even the sound of it whisping through the air was getting me wet. I stared straight ahead at the wall but there was a mirror to the side of the bed. In the reflection, I could only see the side of his body as he moved to whip it across me. I watched the muscles in his arm constrict as he clinched the cane tighter just before he swung it. My whole body would tense up in anticipation as I waited eagerly for it to sting me. When I received each lashing, I'd inhale deeply once and then release a few quick breaths. After about halfway through, perspiration formed on my forehead. I thought I was going to pass out for a moment. He must have given me 100 lashes. He even lashed me across the back of my thighs. I had welts the next day but at the moment it felt wonderful. My entire body was tingling and trembling with excitement.

After he was done, he just took me by the waist and made love to me. He made me get on my hands and knees but by the end, he was on top of me. I just clung on to his neck and savored every last second of it. Our bodies were heaving back and forth in a sweaty frenzy. I usually can't orgasm from sex but he had his hands all over me and I climaxed several times. By the end of it, I knew that he was the one. I only hoped he was feeling the same thing.

Q: Was he the one?

Basima: I don't know. We've been dating for almost a year. We've talked about marriage but I have no idea how my family would feel about it. At this point, they think I'm just crazy and they don't want to be embarrassed by me. I don't really care. Marriage isn't that important to me anymore. Kiran knows that he has never met a woman who raises hell like I do and he likes to lash me as much as he likes taking me out to dinner. I think that's about the most anyone like me can hope for in this world. I don't know if it's a cultural thing but there's something about the feeling and thought of the cane that is especially evocative to me as well. It forces all kinds of memories out of me in a very deep way. Whenever I am traveling in a place and I pass a river with thick stalks growing on its edges, a warm tingling sensation instantly flows through me and I grow really horny. That's just how I'm made.

Kaylee T., *Buffalo, New York*

Q: Tell me about your experiences getting spanked.

Kaylee: I was just out of college and in desperate need of a job. The economy was terrible and nobody was hiring. I had planned on moving to the city, but I ended up moving back in with my parents. It was awful. Plus, I had massive student loans that I needed to pay back. I had gotten a degree in marketing but after a while I just started applying for any job I could find. One of the interviews was for this collections company in Buffalo. It was basically a huge floor of cubicles filled with low-wage workers making obnoxious phone calls to other broke people all day long asking them for money they didn't have. Before I even stepped into the manager's office for my interview, I was already depressed just imagining myself doing the job. I'm not the type of person to be pushy and demanding with people. I knew it wasn't a good fit for me but I was in dire need of a job so I just told myself that I needed to get hired no matter what I had to say.

When I was called in for my interview, though, and met the manager, I was completely unprepared for how good-looking he turned out to be. I had expected some middle-aged, chubby bald guy but Wyatt, the manager, was young, ridiculously fit, and really intense. He wasn't much older than me and I found out later that his uncle owned the company. I was attracted to him right away which only served to make me super nervous during the interview. All his questions were really direct and my answers were rambling promises of how perfect I was for the company. I think it was obvious to both of us that I wasn't right for the job. When he stood up to shake my hand and thank me for coming in, I knew I had to say something.

197

Q: What did you say?

Kaylee: I told him very emphatically that I knew he was thinking I probably wasn't the best person for the position, but I was really motivated and I was willing to do anything he wanted me to do. After I said it, I realized how it might have sounded. He gave me a really sharp look and I just sat there blushing. At first, he wasn't sure how to respond because he didn't know if I was insinuating something or not. Then he told me that I was right that he wasn't sure I was a good fit for the job, but he wanted to know how motivated I could be made to be. The way he eyed me when he said it was very provocative. There was no doubt that he was testing my suggestiveness. I immediately told him I could be made to be *very* motivated. I wasn't even sure what I was offering but there was something about him that made me want to say whatever I had to say. It was more than just my desperation for the job.

There was another moment of silence as he sized up the situation and continued to eye me. Then, he placed his hands on his hips and told me very bluntly, "You'll need to make the quotas I give you, and if you don't you'll be disciplined." I completely froze when he said it. My mind started racing with scenes of being disciplined and I looked back at him trying to figure out what he was really implying. I had one boyfriend who had spanked me a few times for being "naughty" but it was always kind of playful. For some reason, when Wyatt told me I would be disciplined, I knew right away that he meant he would physically discipline me. It was just my sixth sense. I felt like I was reading his mind.

Q: So how did you respond?

Kaylee: Well, after I managed to take a breath, I laughed nervously and tried to gather my composure. I looked down as I tried to figure out what to say and he immediately asked me, "Would that be a problem?" I glanced back up at him and he was staring at me with this really intense look. I mumbled, "No, no, that wouldn't be a problem. I'm fine with being disciplined." I tried to say it in a casual way like it was a normal interview question but we both knew my response was loaded with willingness. He gave me a subtle grin and I tried to suppress my smile. I still didn't know what exactly I was agreeing to but there was no doubt that there was suddenly something more personal between us. He extended his hand once again but this time welcomed me to the company. I stood up, shook his hand and then he led me out of the office. His secretary gave me all the paperwork and I started the next day.

Q: And how did the job go?

Kaylee: As expected, I was terrible at it. I would spend a whole day calling people and not a single one would agree to pay their debt. I'd try to be really nice and ask them when they thought they would be able to pay, but they would give me a nice answer back that was really vague. After the first week, I had only gotten three people to make a payment. On Friday afternoon, Wyatt called me into his office. He gave me a very cold look as he motioned for me to sit down. He immediately told me that I was the worst performer that week. I tried to apologize and promised I would try harder, but he just cut me off. He simply said, "You'll need to stay until seven today. Understand?" Our eyes met and I knew right away what he meant. I felt faint and all I could do was nod up and down in agreement. He said, "That's all. Get back to work." I stood up and scuttled out of his office.

Kaylee: I watched as everyone trickled out of the office at five. I was still calling people at five thirty when I saw Wyatt's secretary stroll toward the elevator. It was the kind of place where employees didn't really talk to each other that much so I don't think anyone even noticed that I stayed late. I was so nervous. As I tapped away at my computer in the empty office, I could hear the sound of my fingers striking every key like it was the loudest sound in the world. It felt like an eternity until it reached seven o'clock. Finally, I gathered my things, shut down my computer and headed to his office. I knocked on the door and he told me to come in. He was still doing work at his desk and he didn't even look up at me as I entered. I closed the door and sat down in the chair opposite him. After a couple of minutes of awkward silence, he suddenly looked up at me. He stood up and walked around to where I sat.

He said to me, "You finished at the bottom of the payment list this week. Do you have any explanation before I discipline you?" I didn't really know how to answer. It was so exhilarating being in a work situation and to have that kind of sexual tension. I still wasn't certain what he was going to do and if he was going to do it right there. I shook my head and told him, "No, I have no excuses."

He told me to stand up as he motioned me with his hand. I rose from my chair and straightened the skirt I was wearing. Then he wrapped his fingers around my arm and moved me behind the chair. He told me to bend over the back of the chair and place my hands flat on the seat. I could feel my heart beating through my chest. I couldn't believe this was happening. I only hoped that everyone in the office was really gone.

After I bent over, I suddenly felt so vulnerable. Even being in that position was like a ritualistic submission to him. When he began to prepare me for the spanking, every movement seemed so real and vivid. He lifted my skirt and delicately pulled it up onto my back. He casually pulled my panties off my waist and then eased them down to my thighs. He methodically rolled the palm of his hand over both of my bare cheeks. He was acting as if it was completely normal for a boss to bring a female employee into his office and give her a bare-bottomed spanking. It was so hot. I loved it.

When the palm of his hand first slapped against my ass, I couldn't help but smile. The first few smacks weren't that hard and they didn't really even hurt. They felt good. But then he repositioned himself, placed his other hand on the small of my back and really laid into me. It started to sting. He moved from one cheek to the other cheek, spanking me harder and harder. He didn't even say anything at all. He just spanked me. The sounds of my bare ass getting slapped echoed through the room. If there was anyone left in the office, they certainly could hear it. I wondered at that point if Wyatt had even thought about getting in trouble himself if someone found out or I were to accuse him of sexual harassment.

He paused for a moment and I just waited bent over in that completely exposed position. I kept my legs taut as I readied myself for more. I decided to glance back at him to see what he was doing. Our eyes met and he immediately noticed that I was smiling. "Do you think this is for your enjoyment?" he shouted at me in this stern voice. I tried to wipe the smile from my face and tell him no, but I couldn't hide the pleasure I was really getting from him spanking me. He immediately grabbed me and started whipping my ass as hard as he could. This time, he just spanked one of my cheeks over and over until I was on the tip of my toes trying to bear the pain. It really did hurt. I began to make noises and gasp in pain.

Then he moved to the other cheek and whipped it in the same way. He seemed to enjoy doing it so hard that he could visibly see me react. After a series of really forceful smacks, I would end up on the tips of my toes or trying to squirm away from his grasp. Even then, though, I was getting totally turned on despite the pain. He finally stopped, lifted up my panties and pulled down my skirt. I stood up and turned toward him. He tried to give me a stern warning to work harder or he would spank me again, but I couldn't help but smile. I muttered to him that I would do my best. There was an awkward silence and then he just opened the door for me. I picked up my things and slipped out.

Q: What happened after that?

Kaylee: I thought about the spanking all weekend. All I wanted to do was touch myself and fantasize about him spanking me over and over. I knew I liked it before this happened, but this was the first time I realized I had a real fetish for it. I guess it was always lingering in the back of my mind in all of my sexual fantasies but this definitely brought it out.

When I went back to work on Monday, it was the only thing I was thinking about. I even wore this short pleated skirt that I thought would invite another spanking. About halfway through the day, I passed by him on the way to the restroom. He simply glanced at me with a polite look on his face. I smiled at him but he didn't seem very receptive. I was totally confused. I knew he liked spanking me. I mean he was the one who had initiated the whole thing.

By the middle of the week, I had hardly made any improvement at in my work performance. I tried to be more aggressive on the phone, but people would just hang up on me. I just wasn't any good at it. Plus, the only thing on my mind was getting another spanking at the end of the week from Wyatt. I wanted to show him that I was trying harder but not hard enough to avoid another discipline session.

On Friday afternoon, I was in the middle of a phone call, when I suddenly sensed someone standing behind me. I looked around to see it was Wyatt. He stood there listening to me which only served to make me incredibly nervous. The person hung up on me and I turned meekly around in my chair to face him. I mumbled an apology and then bit my lip in this really teasing way. I was trying to communicate to him that I wanted another spanking without it being too obvious. Instead, he bent down and whispered in my ear, "I've decided to change your rules. From now on, you'll only be spanked when you get a payment. Is that clear?" I guess I had made it way too obvious how much I liked the spanking and that I would never be motivated to not get more of them. I nodded up and down, telling him it was clear. He gave me a knowing glance and then walked back to his office.

There were only a few hours of the workday left and I had been expecting to get another spanking for my poor performance. I had been fantasizing about it all week long and I couldn't possibly wait until the following week. I began to frantically call every name on my list and demand that they make a payment before the weekend. Now, each call seemed to be sexually charged with this very real reward dangling in my thoughts. I would tell the person on the phone these scary scenarios about being taken to court and having to pay thousands of dollars in legal fees if they didn't pay that day. I was practically threatening them.

After a few calls, I finally got someone to make a payment. I entered all the info into my computer as fast as I could and then ran into Wyatt's office. When I closed the door, he looked up at me in astonishment. I told him excitedly, "I got one." He congratulated me and we exchanged intense looks. I turned to go back out to the office, but he stopped me. He said, "Aren't you forgetting something?" When he stood up and moved toward me, I was in shock. I asked him if he was going to do it right then with everyone still in the office and he said that he was. I knew then that he had a fetish for it as well and just couldn't restrain himself from doing it right away.

Q: Did he do it right there?

Kaylee: Kind of. He had a small restroom attached to his office. He took me by the arm and led me inside. He closed that door as well, but I pleaded to him that people were still going to be able to hear. He just ordered me to bend over the sink as he nudged me with his hand on my back. It was so exhilarating. There was a mirror above the sink so I could watch him this time. It was incredibly sexy to follow his eyes as he lifted my skirt up and examined me before he started. I was wearing a thong so he didn't even bother to pull it down. This time, though, he playfully fondled each of my bare cheeks with the palm of his hand and gave them a few playful slaps before he really began the formal spanking.

The first time he really smacked my ass, though, it was so loud that my face turned red in embarrassment. Being in that tiny restroom bent over like that made it so vivid. There was no way that the sounds couldn't be heard out in the office. I just wondered how audible they were and if people were looking at each other in shock. Wyatt didn't seem to care, though. He spanked me just as hard as he had the first time. I wasn't even noticing the pain because I was so self-conscious. He seemed to know that and was thoroughly enjoying making me blush. It was as if he was intentionally trying to make it louder and louder each time he spanked me. I could feel the full extension of his palm as he tried to strike the meatiest part of my cheeks. He spanked me nonstop for only a couple of minutes but it felt like an eternity.

When he stopped, he told me, "That will be all, Kaylee. You can come back when you've earned another." I stood up and immediately noticed my flushed face in the mirror. I asked him if I could have a couple of minutes to get a hold of myself but he just opened the door. He said, "No, you can't. Get back to work." In retrospect, it was such a turn-on that he made me do a kind of walk of shame back to my desk but at the time I thought I was going to faint. He ushered me out his office door and a couple of other workers immediately looked up at me. I simply put my head down and rushed back to my cubicle. When I picked up my headset to make another call, my hands were still shaking. It was such a strange thrill. I had that warm tingling sensation in both of my cheeks.

Q: What happened after that?

Kaylee: It became a regular thing. The next week, he did it four different times. On one day, he did it twice. It felt so illicit and I was sure we were going to get caught each time.

205

It was like our hidden kinky ritual. I would simply get up from my desk, casually walk into his office and quietly close the door. I would then proceed to bend over the sink in his office restroom once again. He would methodically bare me, spank me until my butt was bright red and then send me back out to my cubicle. It was so invigorating and it made me so horny. Sometimes, I would slip into a stall in the restroom and give myself an orgasm.

Q: How did the relationship go after that?

Kaylee: It didn't. I mean we never really talked apart from work. There was no relationship. I know that he was seeing someone because I overheard him on the phone one day, but neither one of us tried to initiate anything outside of the office. I was definitely attracted to him, but I was hesitant about getting involved with him. I mean I really did need the job on top of not wanting to ruin what we had going. Unless I wanted to seriously be some kind of whistle-blower to the fact that my boss was spanking me in his office, he kind of had all the power. And I liked that. It was intoxicating to be under his thumb like that. It definitely brought out my submissive side in addition to my deep desire to be spanked.

Q: So how long did it last?

Kaylee: About six months. I finally saved up enough money to move to the city. I really could have left sooner but I got used to the dynamic. It really made me wake up looking forward to going to work. Every job I've had since has been kind of dull in comparison. I always ask my boyfriend to spank me but it's different. Getting it like I got it in that office was special. It was like getting spanked in front of a room full of people.

Jin K., *San Francisco, CA*

Q: Tell me about your experiences getting spanked.

Jin: I had spanking fantasies even when I was young. I can't remember the first time I saw someone get spanked. It must have been on TV. I didn't see anything in real life but as I got into my teens I started to notice images of it online or in movies. It sent a weird feeling through me and the fantasies got stronger.

Q: What was the feeling behind the fantasies?

Jin: There was always this urge in me to feel wanted in a very real way. It probably goes back to the fact that I was adopted. My parents were very good to me. Very loving and nurturing. But I think there was always that distance between them being my real parents and them just taking care of a child out of a generic sense of love. I had a lot of trust issues when I was a teenager. I would end friendships with people if they were disloyal to me in the smallest of ways. I just needed a connection to someone that wasn't halfway or was made out of a sense of their own needs. Spanking, somehow, was how I fetishized that need in a physical way. There was nothing uncertain about a man furiously whipping a woman's bare ass. It was real and my door into kink.

Q: Your door into kink?

Jin: Yes, being spanked was the strongest thing for me but as I got to know the world of dominance and submission, my eyes opened up to the full panorama of fetishized desire. I became totally obsessed with it. I watched videos on kinky porn sites, made profiles on online BDSM sites and fantasized constantly. I think about spanking every day but I long for it to be at the center of a real relationship. I want to find someone who I can give myself to and would want to acquire me as his own. There has to be both the mental and physical aspects.

I started meeting men online and exploring the more physical aspects of it once I got to know them. I would ask them to spank me, hold me down and be physical with me in general. But it was difficult to really feel the physical aspect without that mental connection. I need them to be totally into me for the spanking to mean anything. I'd really like to find someone who wants to completely control me, and is strict and forceful, but is still respectful of me. I love the authority aspect of dominating and submission and feeling someone's power over me. He knows how to hurt me, punish me, humiliate me, and make me beg...and knows I love and need every second of it. But I also want the whole vanilla world—going out to eat, staying in to watch movies, enjoying a glass of wine together, traveling to exotic locales—all of that. It's really hard to find.

Q: Have you found it?

Jin: I've found elements of it with different men but no one who I connect with on both levels. I'm starting to feel really hopeless. I'm so horny every day. Sometimes, when I'm home alone, I put one of those little pink rubber gags in my mouth and go around like that. I'll fantasize about something I did wrong and spank myself with a paddle. I'm like this super kinky Asian girl locked up in her apartment just waiting for her dashing authoritarian to knock on the door. I don't know what to do. The more I search for what I want, the less I find. It seems better to just put yourself out there and be open to meeting that one man. I don't know. Maybe I have just fantasized about it so much that it is just a fantasy devoid of real life. I don't know if I should date men who I hope will want to spank me or search out men into spanking who I hope will be really into me, and vice versa. I'm so indecisive. I feel like I need a spanking right now just to have something solid to hold on to. It's not fair. I feel like someone put all these intense kinky desires in me but there is no way I can ever hope to have them all satisfied.